Live with the secret.

DOUBLE

Die with the lie.

CROSSING

RICHARD PLATT

WALKER
BOOKS

DOUBLE

CROSSING

Imperial Hotel,

New York

Monday 10 December 1906

Dear Pat,

I can hardly believe I am writing this to you. It will be the last you ever hear from me, and if you write back, I cannot reply. Nor can we ever meet again. The diary that comes with this note will explain everything. It is my most treasured possession — until recently almost my only possession. I am sending it to you because you are my only real friend, and the only person who knows my story and the truth about me. Once you have read this book, please destroy it: I am sure you will understand why. Then forgive me, and forget that you ever knew me. Goodbye, Pat

From your friend,

David

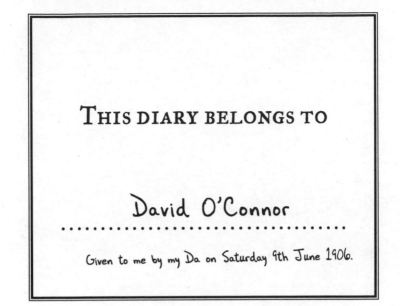

THIS DIARY BELONGS TO

David O'Connor
···

Given to me by my Da on Saturday 9th June 1906.

Wednesday 20 June 1906

Last night Pat and me killed a man! Each time I think about it, I start shaking so badly I can hardly hold a pen. What am I going to do? I desperately want to tell someone about it, but of course I can't, so I'll have to write it down instead.

I never thought I would need this new journal so much. I'm glad of the smaller pages, too, for the one I've been writing in is much bigger. It will be easier to hide this book somewhere nobody will find it.

I pray that God will forgive me this terrible crime, for we hadn't *meant* to do him any harm. We'd just gone down to the lake to look at Patrick's traps. Of course, I knew he was poaching. The fish are not *really* his to take, but the river is teeming with them. Taking one or two to fill an empty stomach does no harm, *so long as no one catches you*.

I slipped out while Da was round the back fetching turf for the fire, for I knew he'd stop me if he guessed where I was headed. I met up with Pat on the corner of Bridge Street. It was unusually quiet and we saw no one. I'm glad of that now.

From the bridge, it's no more than a ten minute walk to the lake-shore – that's why Pat always sets his traps there. We were probably down by the waterside at ten o'clock. It was only the second time I had gone out with Pat – usually Da keeps too close a watch on me to sneak out – and I was scared. Not as scared as I am now, but still frightened enough to keep an eye over my shoulder. If the waterman who looked after the river caught us, I knew we'd be in big trouble.

"Don't be a coward," Pat told me. "Cavanagh's never caught me before. In fact, he's a fat old fool and too fond of his stout to bother with boys taking a few fish at night."

I still wasn't convinced.

The first trap we went to was sprung, but empty. Pat showed me how to bait it and how to pull the springy twig tight to set it. Then we covered the pipe with weed again, and went to the second one.

There we had had more luck. There was a salmon in it. It was a good two pounds. He must have only just been taken, for he beat his tail so hard when I took him out of the pipe that I thought he might slip from my grasp.

I bashed his head on a rock, and then laid him limp and still on some fern leaves.

"Leave the fish there," said Pat. "We'll pick it up on the way back."

I thought at the time that this was a lucky catch, and that we should just be glad of our good fortune, and take it home. If only we had! But I said nothing, for Pat was encouraged by the fish, and eager to see what was in the third and last trap.

It was a little way, and my eyes kept darting back to the road.

Pat saw and said, "What are you looking for? Worried about old Cavanagh?"

"He might be on our trail."

"Then let's give him something else to think about!"

He got a reel of thick fishing line from his pocket, and unwound a couple of yards. He tied one end to a tree, nine inches or so off the ground. Then he laid the line across the track, and wrapped the other end round a fence post, pulling it good and tight before knotting it. Finally he pulled a bit of bracken across in front, to hide the line.

"I'm not sure you should be doing that," I said nervously.

"Oh, don't be such a bore," said Patrick. "It's only a joke. What's the harm?"

But just then I saw a light by the bridge. It could only have been Cavanagh's light. It was the bright, white beam of a carbide lamp. He has

the only one in the town.

I suddenly felt sick and hollowed out, for besides his bright torch, Cavanagh would have his gun. I've never seen him without it. There's even a patch on the inside elbow of his jacket where his habit of carrying the gun in the same place has worn the fabric away.

I looked at Pat, and even in the moonlight I could see he was fearful, though he pretended he wasn't.

"Follow me," he whispered, and we set off along the lakeside as quietly as we could. The track there misses the road, though it is a much longer walk home.

Whenever I dared look back, I saw the torch beam

dancing its way down to the water. It paused at the first trap. The waterman must have known all along about the traps, and been waiting for us to return. What fools we were! My terror grew and I urged Pat on.

I guessed what would come next. I wasn't mistaken. When he reached the next trap, and the bloody fish, Mr Cavanagh let out a bellow. The torch swung up towards us, and its beam caught us before we could duck.

We'd come to a fence, and my jacket snagged on the top strand of tangle-wire, so that I fell into a peaty pool. I could hear Cavanagh crashing along the track behind us. He was close.

"I know you boys," he cursed between his gasps

for breath. "O'Connor [gasp], I caught your father [gasp] and you can be sure I'll get you! Then I'll teach you a lesson you won't forget in a hurry!"

He stopped, and I heard a mechanical noise, like a click or a snap. Then came a flash and a bang, and shotgun pellets hit the leaves above our heads. When I realized neither of us was hurt, I crossed myself and pushed Pat forward. I could hear the waterman setting off again after us. He was wheezing so much now that he no longer had the breath to shout. Pat turned back to me. His face was white and, like me, he was shaking.

"D-d-don't worry–" he stammered– "his foot will surely–"

Another shotgun blast stopped him. This time no pellets flew past us. I turned back to see the light wheeling in the air. It fell to earth and went out. Then silence.

Pat stared and listened for a full quarter of a minute. A vixen barked in the distance, but there was no sound nearby.

"Come on!" he said and we ran. At least *he* did. I could barely work my shaking legs enough to move my feet. This time we went straight back to the road, and home.

Pat was lucky: he slipped in the way he'd come

out, through an open window. But I couldn't. My da was waiting for me. He looked at my soaking clothes as I came through the door, picked up the strap and grabbed me by the collar.

"You've been out poaching–" he shouted, as he swung the strap– "with that thieving lad Patrick!" And again the leather stung my back. "Don't you know what will become of you if you are caught?" And once more. "I spent thirty days in Cavan gaol–" But now the effort of it made him cough so much that he couldn't carry on, and through this I was spared a worse beating.

Da is a fair man and only beats me when I've done something wrong, which isn't often. He thinks Pat is a villain, but Pat has been a good friend to me, and is always there when I need his help.

This time, though, I think we both need help. I don't even care about getting the strap. The pain on my back is nothing compared to the fear in my heart.

Thursday 21 June

I've hardly slept for two nights through worrying about what has happened. When I did sleep, I had nightmares. I was running from something unseen, silent and evil. And though I ran as fast as I could, it wasn't fast enough. I was just about to be caught, when I woke up, soaked with sweat and my heart racing.

I couldn't wait to talk to Pat, but he wasn't at school yesterday, so I called for him on my way there this morning. "Say nothing," he muttered before I could open my mouth. And on the way he added, "We'll talk tonight. Be by the big willow at eight."

So I went through the whole day aching to talk about it, but unable to say anything.

When I got home, Da was waiting for me. At first he said nothing. He just scowled at me as he went about the house. It was awful, for he's always talking, and I almost thought being beaten was better than the silence.

Finally, he spoke.

"They found Mr Cavanagh dead, David," he said, and showed me the *Meath Herald*.

Da pointed to the story and stared at me.

"Was it you?"

I shook my head.

"Was it Patrick?"

I shook my head again.

"But Cavanagh was after you?"

I nodded, "We heard the gun, and then he stopped chasing us," I said.

Da raised his eyebrows. "I heard the gun myself, on my way back from the field. There was a fox barking, and I'd gone to make sure the chickens were locked in tight." He looked back at the paper. "The old fool never knew which end of the gun goes bang."

A second later, he waved the article at me again. "It says 'Orangeman' not 'Waterman'. What does it matter that Cavanagh was a Protestant? Unless the garda think a Catholic pulled the trigger. And if they do, they'll be round here in a flash to know what I was doing on Tuesday night."

ORANGEMAN FOUN
SHOT NEXT TO RIVE

Waterman George Cavanagh, aged 68, was found dead close to the River Dromore on Wednesday morning by a man walking his dog. He had died of a shotgun wound to the head. His own weapon lay nearby. Both barrels had been discharged.

A representative of the garda revealed that they had not ruled out foul play, and added that detectives from Dublin would be travelling to the area to assist local officers. A householder who lives near the death scene confirmed that he had heard two shots the previous night.

The deceased lived alone and was unmarried. His employer described him as "a diligent and enthusiastic waterman and gamekeeper who will be hard to replace". The late Mr Cavanagh was a longstanding member of the local Orange Lodge. The Grand Master there said that the Lodge would "be holding a memorial service for this respected member", but declined to give a date, noting that an inquest will be held.

CHURCH WARDEN'
PARADE FURY

He put the paper down.

"Fortunately, I saw Mr Lang, the pastor from the Protestant church, on my way back from the field on Tuesday night. We'd both heard two gunshots, and were wondering what anyone might be shooting at night. He'll speak for me, but it'll still be trouble. As if I haven't got enough to worry about…"

I nodded. I was glad that he knew, for I've always told Da everything. But I was still shaking with fear that he might ask me exactly what happened.

He didn't. He just looked at me from the corner of his eye and said, "You didn't go out that night, did you, David?"

I shook my head.

"You did your school work. Then you went to bed, didn't you?"

I nodded, and he said, "Where were you on Tuesday night?" I repeated what he'd told me and he nodded and said, "We won't speak of this again."

As it approached the time I had arranged to meet Pat, my da was sat by the fire. He didn't look well at all. I was worried about him, for he's usually such a strong man. I wanted to stay with him, but I *had* to see Pat.

Da seemed exhausted. He'd stopped coughing, and was sitting still in his chair, so I guessed he was asleep. I thought I could creep out without waking him, but as I lifted the latch he said, "David, you wouldn't be thinking of slipping out to meet that youth, would you?" So again I couldn't talk to Pat.

Friday 22 June

While I was at school today the garda called at our house and quizzed Da. He was furious as he told me what they had said…

"The garda made me repeat the story over and over again in different ways, trying to catch me out in a lie. I told them about meeting Mr Lang, and they went away to see him. When they came back they told me it was lucky I hadn't met the priest from our church instead. Do you know what they said to me, David? They said that all Catholics were liars and that we stick together and lie for each other. And then they said that if it hadn't been for the pastor's word, they would have taken me down the station and beaten the truth out of me. How dare they! 'You're a convicted poacher,' they said, and 'Getting revenge on old Cavanagh, were you?' they said. It's enough to make me want to — "

Telling me this story set him coughing again. But

then he muddled my hair with his hand, smiled, and said, "But thank God they didn't ask where you were that night. They're saying it's murder, David."

I jumped when he said the M-word. It was there again on the sign outside the newsagent on Bridge Street: DEAD WATERMAN: GARDA SAY IT IS MURDER. I crossed the road rather than walk past it.

When I saw Pat I told him about the garda's visit, and how they had threatened my da.

"The garda came to our shop, too," said Pat, "while I was at school. They talked to my dad. They asked him what he knew about Mr Cavanagh and how he died. Of course, he knew only what he'd read in the paper and from listening to folks' gossip in the shop. He told the garda it was probably a Catholic that did for Cavanagh, for they had good reason. The garda asked him to explain what he meant. My dad said Cavanagh hated Catholics. He took care to put Catholic poachers in jail. He'd look the other way, though, if an Orangeman who was short of money took a fish or two."

I began thinking what would happen to my da if the garda took him away to prison.

Pat saw the fear in my eyes. He misunderstood and said, "But we weren't there. That's right, isn't it?"

I nodded.

WATERMAN: GARDA SEEK KILLER

Cavan garda revealed yesterday that they are treating the death of waterman George Cavanagh as "suspicious". A spokesman for the force stated that they had eliminated both accidental death and suicide, but repeatedly refused to confirm that a murder investigation had begun. "We are not ruling anything out," he said.

However, a source close to the force told the Herald that detectives had photographed the death scene, and had taken away "certain objects".

A forensic pathologist has completed a postmortem examination of the deceased, but his office would not give details, and would only say that the results would be made public at the inquest, which will be held on the third of next month.

"Good," he said, and pulled a half-smoked cigarette. from his pocket. He lit it, but didn't offer it to me, for he knew I'd say no. He took a deep breath of smoke and blew it out. Then he leaned towards me.

"You know that we would swing if they caught us, don't you? Even though it was an accident. Listen–" he continued– "we must never, *ever* tell anyone we were there, for it will be worse for us if we do. And if one of us is caught, we say we were alone, right?"

"Of course," I said and nodded, though what I really wanted to do was to run away as far from here as I could.

I *am* awfully fond of Pat, but sometimes he frightens me. He's not wicked, but he's determined that we won't be caught and punished for the waterman's death. It's almost like a game to him. He doesn't feel guilty for killing Cavanagh, any more than he would feel guilty for snaring a rabbit in the woods. If I could be more like Pat, I wouldn't feel filled up with fear like this.

I know it's dangerous writing it all down, but I have to tell someone and there is nowhere else I can turn to.

Thursday 28 June – My Da is dead

God has PUNISHED me for Mr Cavanagh's death. HE HAS TAKEN MY FATHER FROM ME!

The shock and hurt of it are almost more than I can bear. Each time I think about writing it down, the pain comes back all the stronger.

I learned of Da's death in the cruellest way, yet nobody was to blame for this apart from me.

Of course I knew he was sick. Not just poorly,

but very ill with the influenza. It had begun with the coughing. Then he was either shivering or sweating. First he would send me to throw more turf on the fire, though the room was already as hot as hell itself. The next minute he was putting off all the blankets and crying for me to open the door and window. I was the same when I had the cowpox that scarred my face with blisters.

All this I remember now with sadness, but at the time… I just thought he would get better, for that was what my da was like. He was always fit and well. He'd never even had a cold.

Looking back, I can see now that I should have known how very ill Da was when he asked me to send for Mrs Foster, Pat's mother, on Monday.

"David," he said, "I'm a little tired this morning. See if Mrs Foster could make us a bite to eat tonight. And ask her to bring me a bottle of something for this cold from the dispensary."

He sent me off to get some money from the tin on the dresser, and I went down the road to the Fosters.

Mrs Foster raised one eyebrow with surprise when I asked her and gave her the money.

"Your father is very poorly?" she said, and it was a question because her voice went higher at the end. I nodded and she said, "Surely I will bring you

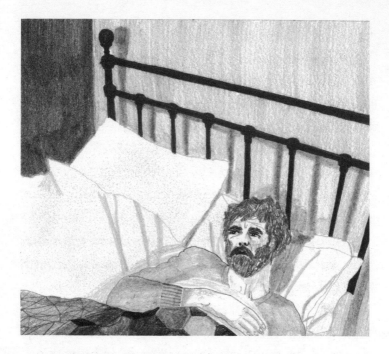

something. Call by after school."

So when Pat and me came back, she took a pot from the oven, picked up a brown-paper bag and came home with me.

Da didn't seem to have stirred from where I'd left him in the morning. Mrs Foster had to shake him to wake him up. Then she propped him up on some pillows. She'd served up a plate of mutton stew and she held it up to his lips. I saw no more than this, though, because she pushed the door shut with her foot. Through the door I could hear the sound of talking, but not the words.

When she came out with Da's plate, it was still full. She told me to sit down, and gave me some stew. It was a lot better than the stew Da makes, and I bolted it down.

While I was eating she said, "David..." and I looked up. She opened her mouth to say something else, but then changed her mind and was silent. She just turned away and wiped her eye.

I know now that I should have asked what she talked about to Da, but I was hungry and I wanted to finish the stew before it got cold.

On the next day, the Tuesday, Da seemed very tired when I came home from school. Pat came by on his bike soon after with his ferrets in his saddle-bag and Rex running behind, tail a-wagging. "Will you come and get some bunnies for the pot?" he said.

I went in to ask Da, but he had heard Pat through the open door. He opened his eyes a little and nodded his head. He pulled me close and whispered that Mrs Foster would be calling in soon to bring him something to eat. Then he smiled weakly and waved for me to go on out. I did just that, and rode off behind Pat, for I thought Da would never send me out if he was really bad.

The warren nearest our house has grown too big: you would need a hundred nets to cover all of the holes. The men go shooting there when the rabbits get so many that they eat the grass from the fields nearby. We went to a smaller one further away, among the tree roots on a little mound above the bog. Pat got there long before me, for he's two years older and has a faster bike. The tread on my tyres is worn right away, and I've repaired the tubes so often that there are patches even on the patches.

When I caught him up he was already busy netting all the holes he could find. We ran out of net, so we filled in the rest with mud. Pat had brought some cheese and bread, and we sat under a tree on the mound and ate them before we put the ferrets down. The sun's low rays warmed us. I lay back on the grass and gazed up into the leaves that were the dark green of midsummer. Pat had a smoke, and it seemed like nothing in the world was troubling him. I wished I could be like him – enjoying each moment – but I couldn't. I thought about Cavanagh and the garda, and then about Da, and I suddenly felt cold.

We were unlucky with the rabbits. We'd missed a hole and they all fled from this back door. Even Rex couldn't catch them. Well, not quite all escaped, for, after a long wait, one of the ferrets came up with a bloody nose and we guessed that she'd made a feast in the warren.

When I got home, Da was worse. I did what I could to make him comfortable, but it wasn't enough. He was very weak, and had eaten nothing that Mrs Foster brought. I tried to get him to sip a spoonful of the linctus that she'd got from the dispensary, but he couldn't take it. I slept badly that night, for I was listening out for him. I woke up every time he stirred.

My da died on Wednesday 27th June.
The day began – as every Wednesday – with the fishman's cart rattling past our door. The cart's smell and its noisy wheels are always a warning that I'll be late for school if I don't hurry, but on that Wednesday I didn't want to go.

Da seemed, if anything, a little better. When I said I'd stay by his bed all day, he said, "No!" louder and more firmly than he'd spoken for nearly a week. He sat up and swung his legs over the edge of the bed.

"David…" he croaked, but got no further, for the coughing grabbed him and wouldn't let go for almost a minute. When he'd caught his breath he continued, "I don't … I don't think I'm going to make it, David…" but then he tried to make light of it, so I didn't really understand what he meant.

I can see now that he was trying to make it easier for me. And that he wasn't joking at all.

"I've written to my brother in New York. If anything happens to me, David, there'll always be a home for you there." He patted me on the head, like he always did. "Don't worry," he told me. "Everything will be all right. You get off to school."

I know I should have stayed with him. The way his eyes were dull and sunken; the way he flopped back into the bed, exhausted. But my father had never told me a lie. When he said everything would be all right, I believed him. I did as he told me. I went to school.

Wednesdays are different from other school days. On Wednesday mornings an Englishman called Birch takes the place of our class teacher, who has to go into Cavan. Even on the hottest days of summer, Mr Birch's gaze chills our small schoolroom, making me wish I'd dressed in warmer clothes. We are all on our best behaviour. Even Liam Genockey sits without fidgeting at his desk, instead of constantly tapping his fingers, as he does every other day.

So when Mr Birch received a note *that* Wednesday, and called out my name, I couldn't help but shiver. What had I done wrong? I could think of nothing that the old man could *possibly* know about. Though pride is a sin, I know I am reckoned to be a good student, and more skilled than most with a pen or paintbrush. I have good marks in all my school-work except divinity. Anyway, I've heard Da call Mr Birch a "godless pagan", so I guessed that my ignorance of the Gospel wouldn't count against me.

The Friday before I'd glued a stag beetle to a thread, so that I could watch it make wide circles in the air like one of the new flying machines. But I set it free the next day, so *that* couldn't be my crime.

Susan McKeever had promised *never* to reveal what I had shown her in the coal yard by the railway station, and I felt sure she wouldn't sneak on me. So I was puzzled to know why Mr Birch had picked me out, and nervous, too. When I stood up, I noticed that he spoke to me in a way I hadn't heard before.

"Come outside with me for a moment," he said. His voice, usually gruff and bullying, was quiet and low. When he rose from his seat, he stirred up a blizzard of chalk dust that danced in the summer sunbeams. I followed him out of the door, shutting it as carefully and silently as I was able. I had been beaten once for slamming it.

When we got outside, Mr Birch did something quite astonishing. He took a linen handkerchief out of his pocket and spread it on the school steps. Then he sat on it, so that his face was level with mine.

I remember his words as if he was standing here now. "David, I have some bad news to give you…" he said. "It shouldn't really be me telling you this but … it seems that there is no one else to do it." He broke off for a moment, and looked into the distance.

When he turned back, I saw that his eyes were glistening so much that I could see my face reflected in them. He swallowed hard, and began again "David, your da … your father. Your father is dead, David. I'm really sorry, lad."

I took a step away from him. I had to grab the handrail to avoid falling down the steps. The ground beneath my feet swayed and rocked as it did when I stepped from the rusty, squeaking iron roundabout in the school playground. The trees and the hills in the distance tilted and shuddered. The normal, everyday sounds of the school echoed far away. I felt as if all the breath had been sucked out of me, and it was a moment before I could speak.

"You're wrong," I shouted when I got my voice back. "It's a lie!"

It simply wasn't possible. My father had seemed better when I'd left him. How could he be dead?

I turned and leaped down the steps in one bound, spun through the school gates and sprinted the short distance home. For some reason I'd expected that the house would look different, that my father's life had somehow turned the stones of the walls and the thatch of the roof into living, breathing things. But from the outside the house looked just as it always did, apart from the bundle of people outside the door.

A forest of arms reached out to bar me from my own home.

I squirmed through, but Dr McQuaid was in my way.

"It's David, isn't it?"

I nodded.

"Now, David, I'm really sorry about your father—" he said— "but I have to ask you some questions before I can sign the death certificate."

I wanted to see Da. I tried to push past, but the doctor's bulky body blocked the narrow doorway. He pulled out a handkerchief from his pocket and dried my eyes.

"How long had your father been ill?"

I gave up trying to get past, and on my fingers counted the days since Da had first sent me down to the big field to feed the cattle. I had struggled to lift the bales of hay, which is why he usually did it. "I think it was eight days," I told Doctor McQuaid. "Please can I see Da now?" I'd seen dead people before at funerals, and I wanted to tell him goodbye.

"I don't think that's a good idea, David," he said. "Now, do you remember what was wrong with him?"

I told the doctor what had happened. "Da caught a cold. I can't remember him having one before. It got worse after he got soaked in a rainstorm; he seemed terribly tired and weak, and didn't want to eat anything." Then I tried one more time. "Please, I want to see my da one last time."

The doctor ignored me. "Why didn't he come to me?"

"Da didn't set much store by doctors," I said, which was true but I didn't tell him the whole truth. I didn't tell him that Da used to call them "quack bone-setters and snake-oil salesmen". Nor did I say that, since our troubles with the farm, we didn't have enough spare money for doctoring, though I think he guessed this.

Then the doctor said, "Your father died of the influenza. Mrs Foster found him. She's a good woman, isn't she? You being Catholics and all?"

For a moment I didn't know what he meant, and I just stared at him. Another tear ran down my nose and dripped onto his shoe.

He dabbed the shiny leather with his handkerchief and explained, "They're Church of Ireland, aren't they, the Fosters?"

I thought about it. The Fosters are our neighbours. I sit next to Pat at school.

The doctor crouched down and spoke more quietly. I could smell his whiskey-breath. "Your father was a God-fearing man. He may not have gone to mass as often as some of us, but he trusted God to care for everything. Too much, perhaps, though I pray the Lord will forgive me for saying it. If he had come to see me, and perhaps eaten a few more meals, he would be alive now."

Then he took my hand, and tried to lead me away. When I struggled, he gripped my wrist hard, and pulled me.

"I want to see my da," I howled, but he was too strong.

A few feet away I saw Mr Foster waiting with Pat. He scooped me up in his arms. I struggled some more and kicked, but he carried me down the lane. I hardly remember what happened then – I was burning with anger and pain – but we must have gone back to their house.

I never saw my da again.

I've been inside Pat's house before, of course, for he's my best friend, and after my ma died, Mrs Foster looked out for me. Sometimes she gives me things to eat at the kitchen table.

Their house is quite different from ours. Instead of a dirt floor they have wooden boards. Some have carpets on them, but they are ragged at the edges. There are curtains at the window, but when you look closely they are worn like the rugs are. The towels are washed thin, though they are cleaner than ours. The main difference, though, is that Pat's house has a staircase. You go up it to reach three rooms where everyone sleeps. Such a thing would be useless in our house. It would only lead to the thatch and the stars. I've never been up the stairs before. Now Mrs Foster told me I would sleep up there, but she only let me up after she'd given me a bucket of water and made me scrub the mud off my feet.

Mr Foster has made a space in Pat's room and laid out a mattress for me. It's a good thing that I like Pat, for he must walk over my bed to reach the door, which now only half opens because the mattress stops it.

We went to bed when it was dark, but I lay awake listening to the wind and the owls calling out to each other. I watched the moon sail across the sky, and missed my da, who I'd never see again. Finally, when the grey dawn lightened the sky, I fell asleep.

At breakfast I asked when I would be going home. Though I spoke loudly enough, Mr and Mrs Foster couldn't have heard me, for they looked at each other across the breakfast table and talked about a house that had burned down at the other side of Cavan, and about whether Linfield or Glentoran would win the football league.

Friday 29 June

The wake and the funeral weren't like others I'd been to. They were much quieter. I didn't expect any of our family to be there because Da's folk are all in America and my mam's family wouldn't come because they blame Da for my Mam dying when she was having my sister. The baby died the next day, too. That was when I began to write journals. Da gave me a book of paper and said I should write down my sadness in it, for he was sad himself, and me telling him my sadness made his worse. There was another reason why he gave it me. He said, "You're clever with words, David, and you're a smart lad. If you practise well, perhaps you can get a good job in Dublin."

But it is my da's death I am writing about, not my mam's. People from the church didn't come to the funeral, because Da didn't go to mass much. He stopped going when Mam died, though he sent me every Sunday; he said it was up to me to decide if there was a God or not.

Some people from the village didn't come to the funeral because my da owed them money. These were the ones who – more often recently – came to the house very angry, with red faces. They shouted at Da, who replied very quietly.

Perhaps there were a few who would have come if the sun had shone. It didn't. And the rain that fell instead would have spoiled their best black Sunday suits.

The stupid ones were afraid they would get ill, for not a week passes here without the *Herald* reporting that influenza has killed more people. No one had wanted to wash and lay out his body, so the doctor himself had to do it. It was the fat doctor who flung the bedding out of the window and onto a fire below.

I watched it burn. The flames roared with such unnatural fierceness that we had to throw water on the thatch, and the stones of our little house cracked with sounds that echoed like gunshots. I cried once more that day.

The wake was a sad affair. There were hardly enough people to pray and keen for my da, so there was a big choice of seats in the church. Besides the priest and the Fosters and me there were five others. One was the doctor, who perhaps came only because he thought we'd leave his fee on top of the coffin, as people sometimes do.

When we came to put Da in the ground my heart felt as if it would burst, though I tried not to cry. But when Mrs Foster pulled me to her I couldn't help but blub, for her frock smelled of lavender as my mam's had when she was dressed in her best clothes. I cried for my da and my lost mam as well.

What am I going to do? I have never felt more alone than I did standing in the drizzling wet by the grave.

Tuesday 3 July

There has been an inquest into Cavanagh's death, which is a kind of trial to work out how someone died. In the *Herald* there was just an inch or two about it on an inside page.

From this small news article I could tell that the garda have discovered very little. This made me feel that Pat and I are a little safer from discovery than we were before.

DEAD WATERMAN: CORONER CONFIRMS MURDER

In the Cavan coroner's court yesterday, Dr Michael H. Taylor held an inquiry with reference to the death of GEORGE CAVANAGH, waterman for the Bellamont Forest Estate at Cootehill, who died on Tuesday 19 June close to the River Dromore. The coroner took evidence from the deceased's employer, from the garda, and from residents of Cootehill. The latter included Owen Callahan, the carpenter who found the body. Summing up, Doctor Taylor stated that, "Cavanagh came to his death by way of a trip line deliberately and maliciously laid by persons unknown, causing the victim to fire his shotgun into his own head." He returned a verdict of murder. Outside the court, a garda representative said the investigation would continue.

Thursday 5 July

I asked again about returning home. This time Mr Foster slowly rose from the table and walked over to the dresser. Opening a drawer he gingerly lifted out a piece of paper. He held it with the tips of his fingers, as if it would bite him, and handed it to me. I unfolded it. It smelled like the sand that they pour on the floor when one of the children is sick at school.

I recognized my father's handwriting – the same neat writing I was used to seeing on notes he sometimes left for me spiked on a nail by the front door.

I folded up the note and put it in my pocket. I took it upstairs to bed with me and put it under my pillow. When I woke in the night, I felt the piece of paper still between my fingers. It made me feel less empty and sad to have something my da had written.

Dear David,

I am writing this now while I still can. If you are reading it, then the worst has happened, so I should say goodbye, my son. I should also say that I love you, which is something I never said often enough, for I thought it was not the kind of thing a man says to a lad.

I want you to know that I am very sorry for what has happened. As I am sure the fat, smart-alec doctor will tell you, I should have sent for him sooner. Now I have left my son an orphan.

In the last few days I've thought hard about what is best for you. Since your ma died, Mr and Mrs Foster have done a lot for us. And yesterday, when Mrs Foster brought some soup, she offered to look after you. This is a kindness I did not expect, that I have not earned, and for which you should always be grateful. But if anything should happen to prevent you from living there, you must go to my brother Dermott in New York. He has a good heart and will look after you with care and love.

Farewell, David, and pray for my soul.

Your loving Da

Friday 6 July

School finished today! I was pleased, because Pat and I will have all the summer together. But I was sad, too, because every summer I can remember I spent helping Da in the field and with the beasts.

In the school-yard there was a lot of talk about Cavanagh and what happened to him. I said nothing and just stared at the hills while this went on, but since I was the only one who was silent Liam Genockey noticed and picked on me: "Maybe it was you, Davey boy? After all, wasn't it the waterman who put your da in Cavan gaol for taking fish out of the river?"

I fought him for this, but he's much bigger than me. He soon had me on my back with my hands pinned to the ground. He would have given me a real belting if Pat hadn't pulled him off and pushed him away. For the rest of the day Liam sat glowering at his desk. Every time I looked at him, he silently mouthed, "I'll get you."

Pat is helping me look after the farm now. We've not bothered with the crops apart from weeding and earthing up a few rows of potatoes that his mam says she can use. The animals still need looking after, though. It was always my job to care for the hens, so I know how to do that well enough. I showed Pat

how to take a stick to bash the rooster. He's an evil brute and always attacks you and scratches your legs if he gets the chance.

I worry about the other animals, though, for Da took care of them. He was always telling me what had to be done, and now I wish I'd paid more attention. The pig we feed on scraps that we collect in a bucket from neighbours who don't have animals of their own. There's plenty of grazing for the four cattle, and I hope that's all they need. I also give the donkey some oats every few days.

Pat and I take our time doing all this. We could be faster, but I like to be out in the fields with him. He's my only true friend, and when we are working together outdoors I forget for a while about Cavanagh, about the garda, and about my lost da.

Sunday 8 July

I am surprised (and a little ashamed) to find that I like living here. It's almost better than living at home. I feel like Pat is my brother, and Mary and Susan are my sisters. Mrs Foster even pretends she is my mam. She kisses me goodnight as well as the other three.

Though I'm happier, the fear of being caught for the death of the waterman still ties my guts in knots. Cavanagh's friends are urging the garda to do more, and today I saw an officer knocking at doors on Bridge Street.

I'm glad I have my diary to write all this in. Pat is the only person in the world I could talk to about it, and he doesn't want to. He pretends we are safe: "They'd have caught us by now if they were going to."

I don't believe him.

Monday 9 July

Pat and I walked past my house today. Since the funeral, it's been locked. The windows are black and lifeless. Outside, nettles, dock leaves and thistles are beginning to sprout from the charred square left by the burning mattress. But today, the door was open and there was a pony and trap outside. I patted the pony eating away in the verge by the gate, and gave it a handful of the longer grass that was beyond its reach.

As I did this, a weasely-looking man came out of the door carrying a book as fat as its owner was thin. He was a stranger to the village, for I'd never seen him before. In the sunlight, he stood and used a fountain pen to add another row to a column of numbers. Then he locked the door using a key tied to a cardboard tag. Dropping the key into his pocket, he walked back to the trap, put his clean, shiny shoe on the step and clambered nimbly in. With a click of his tongue he set the pony off at a trot away from the village.

Seeing the door locked burned me up with a sense of wrong. When I lived in our house, the door had always been on the latch alone. The big rusty key hung on a nail on the wall, but I didn't even know if it turned in the lock. Now the door was locked, and I was locked OUT.

I vaulted over the wall, and ran round to fetch my bicycle, which still stood in the yard. I was too upset to cycle straight back to the Fosters', so I went round the back of the village instead.

It was a mistake. A fox jumped over a wall and darted across in front of me. This gave me such a start that I grabbed the brakes. The worn blocks hardly slowed me. Wobbling and skidding, I slid off the road, buckling the wheel. I fell off and cut my knee badly. I also had to push the bike the rest of the way, but – unlike my home – at least it was still mine!

Thursday 12 July

Today I went with Pat into the centre of town to watch the Orange parade. He told me that it was a grand day and he wouldn't miss it for anything. There's a parade each year but I've never seen it. Since the earliest summer I can remember Da always made sure that we weren't at home around the middle of July. He used to take us to the seaside or the mountains on the twelfth.

"You shouldn't go," said Mr Foster. "There'll be trouble if you do." And he sent me instead to move a pile of turf closer to the house. But his words just made me want to go all the more. So when I finished the task I put on my best green shirt and followed Pat into town. I found him in a big crowd at the top of Market Street.

It began well enough. The men from the Orange order met up by the Church of Ireland that they all go to. For (as I already knew) no Catholics may join the Orange Lodge, which is what they call their club. It was a good-humoured crowd, laughing and joking, for this was their big day. Many of them had large union flags which they waved grandly. The smartest of them who stood at the front were dressed in black suits with orange-coloured sashes or wide collars over them.

Before long a band swelled the crowd. Their peeps and booms and bangs began to echo from the church wall: first in untidy noises that fought each other, then together in a chorus. Its rhythm soon sounded like marching feet, even though everyone was yet standing still.

When the march finally set off we all ran alongside, and Pat knew the words to some of the songs and sang along.

At first it was a fine, jolly day and the sun shone. But I grew tired of the walking. When the crowd set off down the road to Shircock I sat on a wall to rest and lost sight of Pat. The smartly dressed marchers at the front passed me by, and the band, too. Behind them was a crowd of younger men. They weren't marching in step like the others and they were wearing ordinary clothes. Even I could see that some of them had taken a drink or two though it was not yet past noon. Then one of them spotted me. He pointed to my green shirt and lurched towards me. "I've seen you out cutting turf with your da," he shouted. "What are you doing here, you Fenian b——?"

He spat out the words like he really hated me, though he was a complete stranger and I couldn't see what I'd done to make him dislike me. A beery gobbet of slime followed his words, and struck me in the eye. I was so shocked that I fell backwards off the wall. This made them all laugh, and I think it may have saved me from worse, for I saw that some of them had stooped to pick up clods of mud. Another shouted, "Get on home, you poxy-faced Papist urchin."

I turned and ran, with the sound of the drums and pipes ringing in my ears.

When I got back to the house and sobbed out my story to Mr Foster, he called me a foolish lad and clipped me round the ear. But Mrs Foster cleaned the spit from where it had dripped and dried on my shirt, and gave me a glass of milk and a piece of cake.

This made me feel a little better, but didn't mend my wounded pride.

Monday 16 July

My knee has almost healed up from my accident on the bike. Until this evening I had a scab on it, which itched something terrible. Mrs Foster said this meant it was healing up. Sometimes Rex licked my knee, which felt nice, but Mrs Foster kicked him when he did it, saying dogs' mouths were dirty and I should see what they ate. Yesterday Rex was licking away at my knee under the table and he began to nibble at the edge of my scab, which felt good because it was itchy again. I felt a tug at my knee and Rex ran off, chewing and swallowing, his tail wagging. I looked down at my wet knee and the scab was gone, leaving just a pink patch.

Today I went to mass at St Michael's as I still do every Sunday. I go alone, for Pat's family all go to their own church. Today I went to confession, too, for on Thursday I was tired and I'd forgotten to pray for Da's soul. I thought this might be a sin, but when I asked Father Joseph he told me it wasn't, though he said I should keep up with my prayers, for my father needed them more than I could know.

And then I thought about Mr Cavanagh, and wondered if I should confess to what had happened. But the shame and the fear of it welled up in me again, and I couldn't speak of it.

Tonight in bed I talked to Pat about what Father Joseph had said about praying for my da, and he laughed and said, "Does he need all those prayers because he was such a bad man?" and we had a fight. I gave him a Chinese burn and a half-Nelson. I'd never beaten him in a fight before.

"Do you surrender?" I asked him.

"Yes – ow! – I'm sorry. I was only teasing," he said. "What is confession, anyway? They don't have it in my church."

I told him about confession, and how the priest forgives your sins, but he didn't really understand.

"What's to stop bad people doing wrong, confessing their sins, getting them wiped away, then sinning again until next Sunday?" he asked.

I thought about that and couldn't think of an answer, so I told him some other things about our church and he told me all about his, too. We wondered why ladies wear hats in his church, but men must take them off. I fell asleep before we finished, so I don't remember what we decided.

Wednesday 25 July

Yesterday I saw that the paint on the windows of our house had been quickly refreshed. But before it, fixed to the wall, there was a bigger shock: a large printed sign:

That evening, after dinner, I questioned Mr Foster.

"What's insolvency?" I asked him

He didn't immediately answer my question. He took off his glasses, and cleared his throat.

"Your father left no will, David, but that scarcely matters now, does it?"

I was about to ask why, but he continued without a break. "The bank, you see…" And he let out a deep sigh and stopped. When he spoke next, he said his words to the flames in the fireplace instead of to me.

"There's no easy way to tell you this, David. You know your father owed people money?"

I nodded.

"Well, without your mam to help him, the farm lost money."

My da had never told me that. I just knew that since she died, we'd gone without some things that we'd had before, such as tea and sugar, and Da took a drink only on fair and market days.

"Your father bought the farm just before your mam died, David. The Land Commission lent him the money, and he barely made enough to meet his payments each year," said Mr Foster. "He owed money to everybody. Not just to the bank – though, heaven knows, they lent him a lot – but to the grocer, the smithy: everyone. I lent him five pounds, and when he came in the shop to buy things for you, I gave him credit, though I guessed he couldn't pay me. Everything your father owned will be sold. The fields, the house, that bony donkey you're feeding. The whole lot … I'm sorry, David."

Mr Foster talked some more about Da and his debts. I was afraid he was going to say he was sending me to America, but he didn't. At the end he looked down at me and smiled and said, "There will always be a place for you here, lad. The shop isn't doing too well right now, but we'll find a way to make ends meet." Then he sent me off upstairs.

When I got to bed, I shut my eyes and hugged the pillow, and thought how now I have nothing: nothing in the world at all.

Tuesday 31 July

I lay awake last night thinking about our house and the farm and the beasts that would soon all be sold and gone for ever to a stranger. I remembered the weasely man with his fat book and pen. I thought of his smart shoes and how surprising it was that they were shiny, what with all the mud and the dung he would have had to walk through to count our four skinny cows and the donkey and the pig and the hens. And then I guessed … he was a townie from Cavan – a toff and office man – and would probably have jumped a mile if a cow said moo to him.

So at breakfast I told Mr Foster about him, and I mentioned how big the pig is getting. She's about porker weight now, but before long she'll have grown into a baconer, which means her flesh will be fattier and not worth as much.

Mr Foster looked a little puzzled at first, perhaps because he's a shopkeeper not a farmer, but after a moment he nodded and smiled. "Very smart, David. I shall tell the butcher, for he's a good man and can keep a secret."

Sunday 5 August

Pat has helped me fix my bike. With a tiny weeny spanner he tightened up some of the spokes and loosened others so that, very gradually, the wheel became straight once more, and each spoke rang like a bell when he struck it. He showed me how to do this trick, but though I tried three times I only managed to make the wheel more bent than when I started.

While we were doing this, the garda came to the door, which terrified both of us. It wasn't what we feared, but it was still bad news. Someone had hurled a brick through the window of the Fosters' shop on Market Street. The officer had brought the note that was wrapped around the brick. Mr Foster read this, then threw it on the fire without showing it to anyone. He set off to board up the window in a black temper, slamming the front door behind him.

Thursday 9 August

On Monday the butcher came to our farm in the evening and tied up his rope and pulleys to a tree. I helped him and led the pig to him, for she runs to me for food as soon as I come into the field. I opened my mouth to say, "Are you ready?" but he'd already despatched her with his hammer and spike even before I could speak. Just as swiftly he hauled her up in the tree with the rope and cut her neck. I caught the blood in a bucket. I hardly missed a drop, and he said, "Well done, David, that'll make a yard or two of blood pudding."

When the pig stopped kicking I took a look at the hole in her head that the butcher had made. It was small and neat, and hardly big enough for my little finger. I was glad he'd killed her so quickly and kindly for I was fond of our pig. Da would never let me give her a name, and when I said I was fond of her he always reminded me that one day we'd eat her. But I was glad she hadn't suffered.

Today we had roast pork for dinner, and for once we had all we could eat and some left over for sandwiches. Mr Foster has spoken to everyone that Da owed money – except for Mr Anderson from the bank, of course. They have all stopped by the butcher's, so we have at last paid off some of our debts with pork for money.

Friday 17 August

Today Pat and I cycled out further than I've ever been, right round the hills and the lakes. We took a picnic and lay down in the grass above the lake to eat it. We saw some rabbits and wished we'd brought Rex and the ferrets to chase them.

On the way home we rested and took a drink of water on the bridge. I started to talk to Pat, saying, "It's near here that Cavanagh—" but he stopped me short.

"We should forget that ever happened," he said, and stalked off.

I wished there was someone else I could talk to about it. I wondered again if I could confess it to Father Joseph, but I decided that was too dangerous, for someone waiting outside the confessional might hear.

When we got back, Mr Foster said we had ridden thirteen miles. I told him my arse was sore and everyone laughed at me. Mr Foster told me I should say "bottom". But when I said bottom they laughed all the more for I said it the exact same way that he had, so that I sounded just like him.

Last night I heard something I shouldn't have! I knew it was wrong to listen, but I couldn't help myself.

Soon after going to bed, I went to fetch some water. As I came down the stairs I heard strange little gasps of breath. I stopped to listen. Mr Foster was talking.

"Helen, Helen, calm down," he was saying. I waited, straining to hear. I picked out "shop" and "boycott" and "Orangemen". Then, clear as anything, I heard him say, "They told me to get rid of 'that Fenian b——'!"

This made me jump back from the door onto a creaky floorboard, and there was silence for a moment or two. I knew they could only be talking about me. "Fenian" was what they had shouted at the Orange parade. It was a word Da had used only when he came back from the market late, clumsy and smelling of beer. After spending the afternoon in the White Horse Hotel he used to say many things that he wouldn't normally talk about. When I asked him what Fenian meant, it wasn't my da that replied, but the beer. And of course beer doesn't explain things clearly.

This much I understood, though: "Fenian" has something to do with the Catholic church and the Pope and Irish people ruling their own country. My father said "Fenian" proudly, but some people use it as an insult.

When I dared to listen at the door again, Mrs Foster was crying once more, saying, "We can't, we can't!"

Then there was silence. "Well, what are we to do?" Mr Foster asked her. "If he stays here, we shan't have a shop at all inside six months."

At this, I heard him walk across the room, and I fled to the kitchen to get my water. When I returned there was silence from the parlour, so I crept upstairs to bed again.

I wish now that I hadn't heard all this. For though I didn't understand it, I guessed they were talking about me. I seem to be bringing trouble and bad luck to everybody.

Tuesday 28 August

I hardly know how to write what I have just learned. Mr Foster called me into the parlour this afternoon and made me sit down. "You know, David, that you are almost like a son to us," he said. I knew then something bad was coming because at school Mr O'Reilly always says something good to the class when he's about to tell us something terrible.

And so it was. Mr Foster says that his shop is doing very badly. People don't come in any more, and they say it's because they don't want me living here. He said at first it was just the bad people who stayed away. They asked why was he looking after a Fenian b———. He started to say the next word but stopped himself. And then, he said, the bad people threatened the good people and stopped *them* coming. Now a whole day might go past without anyone coming in to buy anything.

Then Mrs Foster opened the door a crack and closed it again quickly but not quite quick enough, for I saw that her eyes were red.

Mr Foster reminded me of the broken window. He said the Orangemen had said sorry, and it was done by bad sorts: thugs and hooligans and not their people, who are all good. And they took up a collection at the Lodge meeting to pay. And then Mr Foster spoke louder and said, "But only half of them gave anything. They had to pass the hat around again for there wasn't enough money for the glass and putty!" And he banged the table with his hand.

Then he sighed and sat down. He wouldn't look me in the face.

"I can't go on like this, David," he said. "I'll lose the shop." There was another pause. "Now don't be upset, but I've written a letter to your uncle Dermott in New York, to ask if you can stay with him. He has replied to say we should send you over as soon as possible." He sighed again. "We don't even have the money for your fare. I'll ask the priest to take up a collection at your church a week on Sunday for it. I shall have to go into Cavan to buy the tickets, so I suppose you will take a ship from Queenstown a fortnight or so later. I am so sorry, David, but you just can't stay here with us."

I can't write any more, for I am so choked with this news. In the space of a few months, I have lost my father, my home, and now I am to lose my country, too. I am become a penniless, unwanted, inconvenient orphan.

Tuesday 4 September

I walked out with Pat this morning. We collected hazelnuts and blackberries and found mushrooms as big as dinner plates. We talked about me leaving.

It was misty and damp and a drip formed on the end of my nose. I think Pat thought I was snivelling when I wiped it away, for he flung his arm across my shoulder and said, "Come on, I'll miss you a lot, but it won't be as bad as all that! You can write to me, and I can write back as best I'm able to –" he laughed and let me go – "which is not very well!"

Then he offered me a cigarette, and it was my turn to laugh, for they are so hard to get that he never offers a whole, unsmoked one to anybody. And though he knew I didn't want it, I knew it was the kindest thing he could think of to do.

"And New York will be exciting," he said. "Don't they have tall buildings called sky-scratchers there? And moving pictures? And flying machines?"

The more he tried to cheer me up, though, the more miserable I felt about leaving. We walked back in silence. Our harvest was so heavy that we carried a basket-handle each to share the weight.

Tuesday 11 September

On Sunday last the church took up a collection for my fare and benefit. It yielded just five pounds eight shillings and fourpence-ha'penny. Among the coins were some foreign ones and even a button. What they have gathered will scarcely buy my ticket to America. Mr Foster says he will pay the cost of my rail fare to Cork from his own pocket. Mrs Foster says times are very hard for everyone and that nobody has anything to spare. People are spending less in the shop and those who give buttons do so because they are ashamed to be seen putting in nothing.

Friday 21 September

My ticket has arrived! The postman brought it today in a fat, stiff, brown envelope. I am to sail on the RMS *Campania* on Saturday. ("That's smart," Mrs Foster said when she saw the ticket. "Isn't the *Campania* one of the fastest liners?")

As well as my ticket, there is a colourful leaflet showing the liner. There are descriptions of the public rooms for first-class passengers, which sound like palaces. First-class cabins seem as big as houses. The description of a second-class cabin makes it sound cosy. There is not much said about the kind of cabin where I will be travelling (on the ticket it says "steerage"). It says only that "there is also accommodation for 1,000 third-class passengers".

To catch the *Campania* I must leave on Monday morning on the twenty past ten train. I will need to change at Ballybay, and at Dublin, of course, and once again at Cork. On Thursday I might have caught an express that goes all the way from Dublin to Queenstown. However, it goes at six in the morning, so this would have caused Mr Foster the extra expense of a hotel in Dublin.

"I just don't have the money, David. I'm sorry," he told me.

Mrs Foster has written the train times on a piece of paper for me. She put this in an envelope and slid it into my coat pocket with a grin and a wink, saying, "You won't need this until you are safely aboard the train." When I sneaked a look later I found (as well as my train times) a one-pound note. It is more money than I have ever had before, and it made me realize that I *really am* leaving.

I have little apart from this money to take with me on my journey. I have my da's gold watch, and a pad of paper and a set of pencils, which he gave me last Christmas. I put these things with the best of my clothes in a dusty canvas bag that I found in the attic here.

Nor have I much to leave behind. I had a few toys in our house, but it seems that these were

First-class cabins

Experience the voyage of a lifetime in the most opulent passenger accommodation in the world.

STATEROOMS

The handsome ensuite staterooms are located on the Main and Upper Decks. Large, well-lighted and elegantly furnished, they are luxuriously equipped for your personal comfort. The Steward's department can be contacted by means of electric bells, and they will be happy to attend you.

LEISURE ACTIVITIES

As well as illuminated decks for your day to day promenades, there is a charming and well-lighted Drawing Room and homely Library which offers you a pleasant and cosy fireside. You may also enjoy a soothing pipe in the Smoking Room.

DINING

Our exquisitely decorated Dining Saloon is the finest room on the vessel. This spacious and elegantly furnished saloon offers passengers the delicacies of the season as well as the finest wines and liquors.

Second-class cabins

Special care has been taken to secure every possible comfort and convenience for our second-class passengers.

We offer a well-appointed Dining Room, Drawing Room and Smoking Room, and a special part of the Promenade Deck is reserved for the exclusive use of second-class passengers.

Meals are served in the Special Dining Room by attentive stewards, and experienced matrons will look after the comfort of women and children.

There is also accommodation for 1,000 third-class passengers. Steerage passengers may be accommodated on the lower deck.

We wish you a comfortable and pleasant voyage.

thrown away by the auctioneers preparing for the sale. That left just my bicycle, which I gave to Susan. She doesn't know how to cycle yet, but Pat will teach her.

Saturday 22 September

Since we learned I would be going to America, Pat has been really kind to me. Last night he said, "Do you want to swap beds until you leave? Mine's softer, and I can put up with the floor for a while."

We didn't swap, but lay talking in the dark about all the things I'd miss most. Then, after a long pause, he said, "Do you want to talk about Cavanagh?" He must have known how much it worried and bothered me. Though I have ached to discuss it with him since it all happened, now that I had the chance at last, I couldn't think of anything to say. I let Pat talk.

"The investigation's got more serious," he said. "To get Cavanagh's chums off their tails the Cavan garda have called their friends in Dublin. They've come up here in smart new suits, led by Inspector Roberts, an Englishman who fancies himself as a kind of Sherlock Holmes." He laughed, then said,

"You'll be in no danger, you'll be gone, and I…" He stopped for a moment and turned on his side to face me. "I'll be all right, too, for no one saw us that night. Ma and Dad don't even know I was out. The only other person who knew…"

"Was my da." I said it for him. "And he's dead."

"I'm sorry, David."

"You don't have to say that again."

"No, really, I am, but listen, what I'm saying is that, apart from you and me there's nobody alive who knows what happened. And if we are both to be safe, we must swear never to tell anyone else."

He gripped my hand in the dark.

"I swear I will never tell anyone."

"Neither will I."

Monday 24 September

I write this on the Cork train.

My leaving from our little railway halt at the end of the line was a noisy affair. The whole Foster family came along to wave me off. Pat rode there on his bicycle behind the trap. All the way Mrs Foster kept reminding me that I had just six minutes to change at Ballybay.

On the platform Pat slipped a ten-shilling note into my hand. It was folded up tight so that nobody might see it passing. I don't know for sure where he got it, but I have an idea, and I'm sure it wasn't honestly. He threw his arms around me and said, "Goodbye," before whispering in my ear, "Remember we swore we would keep our secret."

I nodded. I was too upset to say anything.

When the train steamed away from the platform, Pat ran beside my window, cheering, until he could no longer keep up. I watched him from the window until he was a tiny dot. I wonder if I will ever see him again?

Later the same day – Dublin

It has taken ages to get here, and I'm writing in my diary to fill the time. The Dublin train took hours, even though it travelled as an express much of the way. We went so fast that I put my head out of the window to feel the wind in my hair. I withdrew it when we went through a tunnel, though, for a smut from the locomotive's chimney flew in my eye, and I looked like a chimney boy until I washed.

At Dublin I had to take a tram to Kingsbridge station. Mrs Foster had told me where to go, and to get the tram painted with blue diamonds, but it was still confusing, and I had to ask directions.

The new electric trams are *nailing good*, and far better than those with horses. Of course I climbed the stairs to sit on the top. Each time we came to a junction sparks fizzed in the wires above my head. I think if I'd stood on my seat, I'd have been close enough to touch them.

We rattled along the River Liffey and, as Mrs Foster had told me, I counted off the bridges. I didn't need to, for the huge brewery scented the breeze all malty long before I could see it, and I knew it was time to get off. I had ninety minutes to wait at Kingsbridge, for the Cork train didn't leave until one o'clock. So I sat on my bag and ate one of the sandwiches Mary had made for me. They were egg, and they reminded me of our chickens, and of the farm, and the house, and the green fields and Pat and Mary and Susan, and I ached to go back. I could have sobbed there and then, but I didn't want people looking at me.

The hands of the station clock don't seem to move at all. To take my mind off how much longer I have to wait, I wrote these words in my book, which is starting to seem like the only friend I have left.

Later still – Queenstown

I haven't slept since stepping off the train. I was travelling until long after dark, for I had to change again at Cork, and Queenstown is nearly an hour from the city. A boy from the shipping company met me at the station, and took me in a trolley-bus to a lodging house near the docks. I couldn't sleep. To begin with I was too worried and homesick to even close my eyes. Then I dozed a little on the thin and lumpy mattress, but each time I opened my eyes the very walls of the room seemed to move. Not like at Christmas when I sneaked a drink of stout, and the bedroom walls spun round. This was more of a wriggling, like the surface of a bubbling soup pot. Thinking I must be dreaming, I got up and brushed my hand across the filthy paintwork. All kinds of winged and crawly things skittered over my advancing fingers. After that I crouched on a chair, afraid to touch anything in the room.

Tuesday 25 September

This morning the shipping agent's boy returned for me at around eight. He hurried and shooed me through the drizzle on foot to the dockside. There, for the first time, I saw The Ship.

"Big" is too tiny a word to describe it. This ship is truly ENORMOUS. I've never seen anything like it in my life. If the front end was at the Market Street crossroads, the back of it would still crush the altar up the road in the Church of Ireland. The ship's black-painted side, streaked with red, almost blocked the view across the harbour.

I think Pat's mam might have been wrong, though. The *Campania* certainly doesn't look like the fastest ship on the Atlantic. It has a worn, sad look to it. If it was a horse, it would have a limp and the mange.

There was a ramp on the dockside, which passengers were walking up to board the ship, so I walked towards the quayside to do the same. I didn't get far across the cobbles, though, for a big man pushed me roughly towards a door in one of the dock-side buildings. Beyond was a long room, with a line of waiting passengers. At the far end of the line, sitting at a wooden table, was a tired-looking man with a red nose.

We shuffled slowly towards the desk. The rain had wetted all of us, and I could smell soap on some of the neat families who had scrubbed themselves for the voyage. Those who hadn't brought with them the ripe smell of farms, fields and dung. Coming after the town smells of oil and soot and smoke, I was reminded of the country and felt homesick again.

I finally edged to the front of the line.

"What's your name, lad?" the red-nosed man asked me.

"David O'Connor, sir."

He wrote this down carefully in a wide column on the left of a big sheet of paper that lay across his desk. Then he asked me question after question, filling in his columns.

"What is your age?"

"Are you married or single?"

"Can you read and write?"

"What is your nationality?"

Sometimes I couldn't answer.

"What is your calling or occupation?"

What did that mean?

"I think we shall just put 'scholar', if that's quite all right with you, *sir*?"

He talked to me as if I was a grown-up, but somehow he made every word sound like an insult. He reminded me of Mr Anderson at the bank the few times when I had gone there with Da.

Some questions I didn't understand at all, such as, "Are you an anarchist or a polygamist?" Each time he answered "No" before I could even ask for an explanation, adding, "For if you were an anarchist or a polygamist, you would not be likely to tell *me*, would you, *sir*?"

As he blotted the damp letters, he pointed his pen towards one of two doors behind the desk. It led to a white-painted, brightly lit room where two men were arguing. One wore an old badly fitting suit. The other, who was dressed in a very clean white coat, was saying, "Look, I'm sorry. I don't make the rules. You have ringworm. The medical inspection book calls it a 'loathsome contagious disease' and

Inspection Card

(Third Class Passengers)

Port of departure Queenstown   Date of departure:

Name of Ship ...... Campania ......, 25 SEP 1906

Name of Passenger David O'Conner

Last residence Ireland

Inspected and passed at Ellis Island	Passed at quarantine, port of	Passed by immigration Bureau, port of
UNITED STATES PUBLIC HEALTH SERVICE.	U.	
	(Date).	(Date).
Seal or Stamp of Consular or Medical Officer.		

5   **6**

Berth No.

To be punched by ship's surgeon at daily inspection

you'll never even land in America. The doctors on the ship will put you on the next one home."

When the scruffy man shuffled away, he was in tears. The doctor waved me forward.

"Here's one who won't require vaccination," he said, looking at my scarred face. I wondered what he meant. He quickly tousled my hair and shone a light into my eyes and mouth, pressing down my tongue with the same wooden stick that I noticed he'd used for the man before me. Ugh! Then he gave me a piece of paper. "Get this stamped every day by the doctor on board ship, to show that you didn't fall ill."

I didn't understand this, for I couldn't see how the simple stamping of a card could protect me against disease.

Stepping outside, I got another push, and soon found myself on the ramp that lets passengers onto the huge, waiting ship. It was so windy that I thought I would fall off; the ramp rose up the side of the ship so steeply. Wooden slats crossed it every foot or so to make it less slippy. There were strips of canvas lining the sides but I was still scared I'd slide under them and fall in the ocean.

At the top of the ramp was a red, hairy, giant of a man, with a polished badge that read CHIEF STEERAGE STEWARD. He took my ticket and the certificate the doctor had given me. He frowned down at me over the top of his spectacles.

"On your own, is it, lad? Hmmm, that's a teaser. I think we'll put you in with the families, then." And he directed me to an iron door at the end of the deck.

When I stepped through it, I had a sudden, dizzy moment of alarm. Beyond the door, there were no stairs as I'd expected, but something much steeper. It wasn't quite a ladder – but it wasn't a staircase either. Grabbing the handrail to avoid tumbling forward, I lowered myself into a churning mass of figures. I'd never seen so many people so close together before. It was like a month of market days and the summer fair all rolled into one. All around men swore and cursed and children chattered, Babies cried, and women hushed them. As I climbed down the ladder the hubbub swelled, rolling over me like the surf on Strandhill beach.

I pulled my ticket from my pocket, but it was instantly snatched from my hand.

"Nineteen. That's the top bunk, halfway down." A big hand pushed the ticket back into my pocket, then propelled me across the floor. My feet slithered on the greasy steel plate, and I would have slid right past my bunk if I hadn't grabbed one of the metal tubes that supported it. A ladder led up. My suitcase had raced me there and won.

I climbed the ladder and tumbled onto the lumpy mattress. It felt like it was filled with dried seaweed or straw (the truth, I discovered when I found a hole in the cover, was a mixture of the two).

I looked around me. Besides my suitcase, I shared my berth with: a lifejacket that also served as a pillow; a small, thin, white blanket; a fork; a spoon; and something made of tin that I couldn't identify, but which seemed to be a plate, a cup and a bowl all made as one.

By pushing my luggage to the end of the bunk

and placing most other things on top of it, I could just about stretch out straight. I looked around for a place to stow my suitcase, but there was nowhere. This cramped space will be my home for the next week.

As I struggled to organize my new possessions, the sound of the ship's horn transformed the room. *Before* the blast, everything was chaos: everyone around me seemed to be doing or saying something different, and moving in different directions. *After* the blast on the horn, each was doing exactly the same thing as all the others. All flocked to the companionway (what they called the steep staircase leading up to the deck) like ants to spilled sugar.

I followed them up, but before I'd put my feet on the lowest tread, a low-pitched, regular thumping rose from beneath my feet and I felt the ship begin to move.

Once I emerged into daylight, I wished I'd never gone onto the deck. Every one of my travelling companions was crowding the deck rail, waving and shouting farewells to their family on the quay. I had no one. I looked down at the hundreds of faces and wished that Da or Pat, or Mrs Foster was among them. But of course they weren't.

Everyone was sniffing and dabbing their eyes, but for the first time in days, I didn't feel like crying.

I turned around and looked out to sea, and suddenly everything changed. I may have nothing to leave behind, but I have an adventure ahead of me!

Wednesday 26 September

We left Queenstown harbour a day ago, but until this morning the sea has been very flat. Now, though, it seems that the wind and waves have got together and decided to shake us about a little to see what happens. Our bunk-filled room, already hot and stuffy, now stinks of sick, as many of us haven't been to sea before.

To avoid being seasick, I flee to the deck whenever I can. Even here, there is hardly enough space to stretch out. The deck has been made like a farm, with fenced pens, but here the fences are to keep the steerage passengers from mixing with cabin class. We steerage pigs must fit ourselves where we can. We squeeze between the winches, ventilators and other machines that half cover a small area at the back of the ship. A shower of cinders falls constantly from the funnel above, catching in my hair and eyes.

The lucky passengers in cabin class have paid more and may graze on several clean, open spaces.

Each one is as big as *all* of our farm at home and their decks are protected from the rain by canvas covers.

My escapes to the deck are not lonely. Most of the steerage passengers follow me up. We all prefer the North Atlantic wind and the black snow-shower to the stinking stuffiness of the cabins below. Some of us come up to the deck as soon as we wake each morning. We can only bear to return below to collect food, and when the crew drive us back at nightfall. We would sleep on the cold hard deck if they let us.

I am slowly getting used to the crush of people. When I open my eyes in the morning I see in an instant more different faces than I've seen in my life before. Though I am part of this huge crowd I feel more alone than I have ever felt.

Today I had a strange experience. I was lying on my bunk, my head buried in my coat to try and blot everything out. I thought if I couldn't see anything it would be easier to imagine my home, with the green fields and the little house, and Da. But with each day that passes the picture grows a little paler and less clear, as if fog is covering it up.

A tug on my leg made me open my eyes. I dried them on my shirt sleeve then peered out a little to see who it was and what they wanted. A woman was smiling at me over the edge of the bunk.

"What's your name?" she said. I lifted my coat more. She looked just like my mam. Her hair was brushed just the same, and she wore a scarf over it the way Mam did when she was digging or cutting turf. I liked her immediately.

"David O'Connor. What's yours?"

"It's Mrs Doherty. I'm from Cork and so is Mr Doherty. We have two girls called Marrie and Nora."

Suddenly I have some friends!

Of course I've met many other people in our cabin, and they're all friendly enough, except for one old man who talks to himself. He smells very bad and lies on his bunk all the time. His family even bring him his food to eat there.

They bring it to him in his canteen, which is the name for the lumpy tin contraption that was on my bunk. Each part has its own special use. The base holds soup; into the bowl the steward spoons vegetables, and a stew made from the meat of a beast I've never tasted before. The cup holds tea or a liquid I'm told is coffee. Stewed fruit fills the moon-shaped crescent where I'd found the cup. I have started to spend a lot of the money Mrs Foster gave me on buying food. The free food we are entitled to isn't even good enough for pigs.

Thursday 27 September

Yesterday night I was so sick from the ship's rolling, I could hardly move from my bunk. Nor could I eat anything. This was perhaps a good thing, because I needed my canteen for something other than meals. As there are no other containers in the room, I use the largest compartment to catch the contents of my stomach.

When any of us wants to wash, the same deep bowl becomes a complete bathroom, since there is just one wash basin for every eight passengers, and only one hot tap for the whole room.

I have seen many far worse uses for canteens, but I try not to think of them, for these memories make me want to retch again.

After a night and half a day of sickness, I began to feel a little better. The Doherty girls helped me to start eating again by sharing little portions of fruit, hard-boiled eggs and other tasty food they've brought with them. They seem to have adopted me as a brother. Each evening they sit together at the end of my bunk combing each other's hair. I don't know how I'd survive without them.

This evening we had a fine time in our stuffy cabin. There was a torrent of rain outside, so we had no choice but to huddle indoors. First a rat appeared and for fifteen minutes we chased it around the cabin. This is unusual not because there are few rats (there are a great many) but because this one was so slow and dim-witted. They are usually fast and wily. They come out at night looking for food in our luggage. They drop onto my bunk from the pipe that passes over it and their footsteps on my blanket wake me. At night they skitter away so fast that all you see is a tail. So this dim one came as a surprise. We chased him down, and thought we'd cornered him. However, he slipped away through a hole in the steel floor. The gap is so small that I can barely get two fingers into it.

After we'd collapsed in exhaustion from the effort of our hunt, someone brought out a fiddle, which he played with great skill. On hearing this, another man brought out his bodhrán, and beat out a rhythm on its stretched dog-skin A third had a tin whistle, and a fourth an accordion, which he called a "leather ferret". They played tunes like "Maid behind the Bar" and "Mountain Road" that we all knew well, and pretty soon we were on our feet dancing jigs and reels. It was joyful, but put me in mind of the summer bonfires and dances of Lughnasadh at home, and I moped to bed, dejected. I didn't want anyone to see me cry.

Friday 28 September

I've been so bored today, I decided to explore! I know every corner of the tiny kingdom that we steerage passengers inhabit, but I wanted to go further. Wherever our country touches that of cabin passengers there's a border crossing and closely guarded checkpoint. It's as if we're at war with the ship's other passengers.

In most places an iron bulkhead or locked door separates the two zones, but I was determined to be adventurous in my travels. Yesterday morning I slipped under a rope from which hung a sign that reads FORBIDDEN TO ALL PASSENGERS. Beyond, I discovered a place where a ventilator divides the deck from cabin class. The ventilator is pushed up against the ship's iron wall, but doesn't quite touch it. For an adult, it's a real barrier, but a boy my size can just about squeeze through.

Though I'd got this far before, I didn't dare take the next step and cross into the forbidden world on the other side. Today I returned to the same deserted place, and stared out to sea. I'd been there half an hour, lost in the distant clouds and waves, when I heard someone call out, "David! Pssst! Why don't you come across?"

I whirled round and almost fainted with surprise.

The boy standing on the other side of the ventilator, the boy who was calling my name, was … me!

It was like looking into a mirror. Apart from his clothes, the boy who faced me across the deck could be mistaken for me. Even his face was scarred like mine.

"You can wriggle through," he told me. "Quickly! Nobody will see. The crew only come up here when we're in the harbour, to operate the winches."

I took another look at him. "What's your name?" I asked.

"I'm Jack," he said, "and I know you're David." He held out his hand across the gap. I shook it uncertainly. The only person whose hand I'd shaken

before was Father Joseph at St Michael's, and I'd always found his limp, clammy fingers rather creepy.

"How do you know my name?"

"I noticed you when you came on board, of course, because you look *just* like me! I read the name on your luggage label! Now squeeze through fast, before anyone comes."

I stared at the gap, then at Jack, beckoning me to come through. It was such an easy barrier to cross, but it might just as well have been a rabbit hole he was asking me to crawl through. Everything I have ever learned told me to stay on my side. But Jack wasn't going to squeeze through to reach me, that was clear. The other side offered the promise of comfort, warmth and friendship.

"What if I get caught?" I asked.

"What's the worst that can happen? They'll just send you back to steerage. Anyway, I know loads of places where you won't be spotted."

I stepped forward, put a hand through the gap ... and hesitated. Then I heard a sudden noise behind me. Heavy footsteps clanked on the ladder that led up to the deck.

Jack fled. I pushed myself past the ventilator, and followed him.

When we went inside out of the wind, he shrunk away from me. "Yuck, David, you stink of puke! Do all steerage passengers smell like that?"

I told him what it was like, how the whole cabin stinks, and that when people are sick on the floor, nobody cleans it up. Jack pulled a disgusted face. "Come on, we'll go to my cabin. You can have a bath there. The steward has already made up the cabin. My tutor has found a sweetheart on board, so he's never around. He's all lovey-dovey, darling-this and darling-that. At first it annoyed me, but now I'm glad because I can do what I want."

Together, we slipped down the staircases and corridors to Jack's cabin. Luckily, we didn't see anyone. When Jack unlocked the cabin door I stared wide-eyed at the luxury. In steerage eight people sleep in the same space. Here there were just two beds. I drew my hand across the crisp sheets. The table was plummy: it unhooked and folded up to make more room in the cabin. I took an apple from the dresser: it wasn't as good as the ones I used to scrump from Mr McFarquarr's orchard but it was still delicious.

When I was in the bath, Jack sat on one of the beds, and used his toe to turn over my grubby, creased clothes on the floor.

"Yeuch! You'll never pass for a cabin passenger in these. You can borrow some of mine." He pulled out a drawer, and laid on the bed a clean pair of trousers, a shirt and a sweater.

It took me five minutes to get a comb through my newly washed hair. When that was done I got dressed, and Jack opened a cupboard. There was a mirror on the inside of the door. Reflected in its glass, I saw my own face and Jack's, side-by-side. I watched my own jaw drop. Jack blinked. Then we both spoke at once.

"That's *really* odd!" I said.

"If your hair was a bit neater we'd look like twins," he said, and we both laughed.

I followed him from the cabin. My new disguise

was tested almost as soon as the door was locked behind us. A cabin steward was walking down the narrow corridor towards us, carrying a silver dome on a tray. I froze, but Jack tugged my sleeve to urge me on. The steward flattened himself against the wall to let us pass.

"Good *afternoon*, Master Jack! Where have you been hiding your brother? Did you bring him on board in a big suitcase?"

I froze, but Jack laughed. "No, he's not my brother! We just met. This is David."

The steward grinned. "'E's not a stowaway, then!"

Jack laughed again.

I looked over my shoulder as we walked on. The steward was still standing in the corridor, scratching his head.

After this, we didn't take any more chances. We skulked on decks that the crew and passengers rarely visited. When we did see people, we split up so they never saw us together. This was Jack's idea, and it was a brilliant wheeze: I soon got used to people saying, "Hello, Jack," to me, and replying politely.

At lunch Jack stuffed his pockets with whatever he could, and I ate ravenously. Steerage food is awful; I throw all of my meals over the deck rail into the sea. The food I've been buying with Mrs Foster's money is expensive, so it was good to get a free meal.

As the day ended the sun sank below grey Atlantic clouds. Briefly the ocean ahead turned to gold. Jack and I sneaked back to the cabin, and I changed into my grubby clothes again. Then I vaulted back over the gate and returned to the filth, stench and stuffiness of steerage. After a full day away it smelled more putrid than ever.

What an extraordinary day I've had! Mr Doherty had noticed I was missing.

"Where've you been?" he asked "We didn't see you at dinner or supper."

"How did you get a proper wash?" Mrs Doherty asked.

I mumbled a reply – I didn't want them to know where I'd really been.

Saturday 29 September

After breakfast this morning I ran up to the top deck again and met Jack at the same spot. This time, though, he scarcely looked up when I greeted him. He stared down at the deck and kicked at a loose piece of rope.

"What's the matter?" I asked.

"I got caught, that's what."

"But you hadn't done anything!"

"The steward didn't see it that way. There was a thick grey ring round the bath, and he asked Peter – that's my tutor – what had been going on. I said 'nothing' and got a clip round the ear for lying."

"I'm sorry, Jack."

"It's not your fault," he said. "And anyway, it worked out all right in the end. I had to tell Peter about you, and he really doesn't care. Just says to be careful – and to clean the bath!" Jack grinned now. "So you'll need this…" And he hurled a sodden rag that he'd hidden behind his back. Well aimed, it caught me full in the face. Sputtering and soaked, I chased him down to the cabin.

We spent most of the day there, lying head-to-toe on the bunks or sitting up. When we tired of being indoors, we ran around the windy decks. But wherever we were, we talked, and talked, and talked some more.

Jack told me all about his childhood; his life had been very different to mine, though he's half an orphan, too: "My mam died when I was just two years old, so I hardly remember her." He looked down at the floor for a moment, put his hands in his pockets, then continued.

97

"*Her* father died a week later – Gran says of a broken heart. She told me it was awful: the house was full of people wailing and sobbing. Anyway, after two funerals my daddy didn't know what to do with me. I think I reminded him too much of my mam, which made him sadder. He went to America on business, leaving me with Gran in Dublin. He made two trips to America, then on the third trip he … he just didn't come back. I stayed with Gran in our house on St Stephen's Green. It's enormous. A governess looked after me when I was a little boy, and then Peter."

Jack is just like Pat, only more so, though I know that doesn't make any sense. I can tell him anything, just as Pat and I have no secrets from each other. But there's something more. He has no mam, and neither do I. Even before Da died I always felt like there was a hole in my life. Jack is the same.

I would never be able to explain this to Pat, for he has a mam and da, and anyway, how do you describe it when there's a gap?

Jack even understood when I told him about the Orange parade, though like Pat, he's a Protestant.

He just shrugged and said, "Well, the Orangemen are all *Boom! Bang!* and 'No Popery!', aren't they?"

But then he asked, "Do Catholics pray to Jesus,

like we do in our church?" I was glad I'd stayed with the Fosters, for there was nothing he could tell me about *his* church that I didn't already know. I told him about them and how they had looked after me when Da died. I even found myself telling him how nervous I was of meeting Uncle Dermott. What was America going to be like? Would I make new friends? Would people there know I was a Catholic?

"Why are you going to America?" I asked Jack.

"My father made some money there, and he's got married again, so I have a new mam. She has two daughters, and my dad wants to bring the family together. Peter is taking me as far as New York, but then he has to sail back to England. He'll be a school teacher in a few weeks. We're going to stay in a hotel until my 'family' arrives from the Mid-West."

When he saw my blank look he said, "Don't you know *anything* about America? The Mid-West is like, well, you know what cowboys are?"

I nodded.

"Well, that's where it all happens ... you know ... ranches, cattle, the odd cactus, Indians, outlaws..." He quickly changed the subject. "Tell me about ferreting again. How do you stop the ferret killing the rabbit?"

Sunday 30 September

I awoke last night with a start. Rubbing my eyes sleepily, I thought for a moment that some noise had roused me. However, I could hear nothing – not a sound. But then I realized that it was *the silence* that had woken me up. Apart from the snoring of everyone around me, the ship was quiet. The regular thumping of the engine that has accompanied our journey like a heartbeat had stopped.

As noiselessly as I could, I pulled on a coat and lowered myself down from my bunk. I padded across the floor, crept up the companionway and stepped out into … nothing. The ship's lights shone dimly into fog. It was as thick as porridge and as white as linen sheets laid out to bleach on meadows and bushes. I groped my way a little round the deck until the damp night air began to seep through my clothes. Then I crept back into bed as quietly as I'd crept out.

In the morning the fog was still as thick. Now, though, the ship's horn has started, a mournful howl so deep that I can feel it throb through my chest.

The moist white blanket has made many of us feel anxious. Some complain that as long as we drift in the ocean like this we're going nowhere and our arrival in New York will be later. The fog doesn't worry me, though. In fact, from the moment I stepped out on the deck into that mixture of darkness and whiteness, I had an idea that the fog might provide a chance of some fun.

Before the breakfast bell rang I climbed the ladder to the upper deck without worrying, for once, that I might be spotted. Unless I actually collided with a member of the crew, none of them would see me, even if I was standing just a couple of yards in front of them. At the top I wriggled past the ventilator, and went in search of Jack.

When I tapped gently at the door of his cabin he opened it in his pyjamas. Peter was still snoring in his bunk. I whispered quickly to Jack what I had in mind, and watched a grin spread across his face. Thus began our day of exploration. For with the ship smothered in fog, we can creep unseen onto ANY DECK we choose.

We started with first class. Together, Jack and I strolled arm in arm on the 1st promenade deck as if we were a pair of toffs. He smoked an imaginary cigar and pretended to swing a walking cane. When he imitated the voice of an English gent to ask me the time I was so surprised that I looked over my shoulder. This made us both laugh so much that we could hardly walk for a moment. When we continued, we bumped into a white air vent shaped like a huge mushroom. It loomed up so suddenly from the fog that we didn't see it coming.

Next we decided to see how high up the ship we could reach. We passed more NO ENTRY FOR PASSENGERS and CREW ONLY signs than I could count. We climbed so high that all the sounds of the ship were muffled in the wet, white fluff below us. Well, almost all sounds. For as we climbed, so the fog horn's hoot grew louder. Finally, we reached a warm, curved, red steel wall. I turned left and Jack turned right, and we groped our way along it. Just a moment later I slammed up against a figure in the fog, and fell to the ground. I was terrified that I'd been caught … until I heard my name called through a fit of giggles. It was Jack. "It's the funnel, you mallet-head!"

As if to prove him right, the fog horn sounded again, just above our heads. It shook us so hard that I found even thinking difficult.

When it stopped I heard shouting, very nearby: "The skulking little ragamuffins came up this way!"

We were standing next to a steel ladder, and Jack grabbed a rung and started to climb. He vanished into the fog in an instant. I flung myself up after him, grabbing each rung with my hand as soon as his foot was off it.

At the top of the ladder we stepped right into the funnel, and stood on a small metal platform inside. I gulped in the warm air, clinging to a rail to stop my hands from shaking with fear. We waited there, panting, while the crew searched the deck below. When the fog horn sounded again right behind us I almost jumped out of my skin.

By the time the search had been called off, our clothes were covered in a white layer of moisture, and a drip had formed on the end of my nose.

Jack said, "We've been to the top. Why don't we find the bottom now?"

We clattered down the steel ladder, still sure that the fog would keep us safe. We swanked down majestic, thickly carpeted staircases and clambered down steep companionways. Finally we came to a heavy door marked TO BE KEPT LOCKED SHUT AT ALL TIMES. It was open.

Jack went in first. He seemed fearless, so I forced myself to follow him, but not before looking nervously over my shoulder, both ways, several times. We stepped out onto a metal bridge. This soared across a vast room as big as a tram shed. A strong oily, steamy smell rose from the black depths below us. Through the metal mesh floor beneath our feet we could look down on four giant, hulking shapes painted dark green. Shiny metal shafts the thickness of tree trunks stuck out from them. And all around us was a forest of brass dials. Some were painted with numbers, others marked FULL, HALF, SLOW, STAND BY, STOP and FINISHED WITH ENGINES. A brass arrow pointed to the last of these.

I reached up to run my hand around the brilliant shiny brass rim of this dial, when a booming voice echoed through the silent boiler room.

"Oi! What in God's name are youse two doing down here? Gertcha!"

Accompanying this angry shout was the clanging of heavy boots leaping steel steps two at a time. We fled, falling over each other as we made our way out, then pretending to walk casually away, as if we didn't care about being caught. But when we got back into Jack's cabin, all my clothes were stuck to my skin, and I saw that Jack had beads of sweat on his brow.

We spent the rest of the day curled up there, eating picnics he sneaked from the dining room; and in the 2nd lounge, talking hidden in a corner behind potted palms and stacked chairs.

Jack couldn't believe that I'd never left County Cavan: "You went to Dublin for the first time only

last week? It's not possible! Dublin must be the best place in the world ... apart from Cootehill, of course. I had so much fun there." He talked for hours about his childhood in the city.

Now I know so much about Jack's life that I feel that *I too* lived in his fine house in Dublin's finest square.

Monday 1 October

I've had the most terrible day. I was caught sneaking round the ship, and I'm covered in bruises as punishment for my crime. Worse, I don't know how I'm going to see Jack again.

It began well enough. In the night the engines started again, this time waking everyone up. At dawn circular shafts of yellow sunlight cut across the smoky air of our stuffy cabin from the few portholes.

I met up with Jack in the afternoon. Yesterday's fog had made us bolder, and together we sneaked onto the deck at the very front of the ship. It was brilliantly sunny, and as we leaned over the deck rail the wind brushing our hair seemed almost warm.

Suddenly Jack shouted, "Look!" and pointed straight down.

Right below us, a big black-grey fish with white sides was racing along. It was just in front of the wave cut by the sharp front edge of the ship. I thought it was a shark, but (with a great sigh, as if I was stupid) Jack told me it was a dolphin. Soon it was joined by lots more dolphins. We watched them for ages being pushed along by the ship's wave. Sometimes they leaped clean out of the ocean.

After the wind began to make my ears ache we found a spot out of the breeze and out of sight and — best of all — warmed by an air vent. It was so warm, we didn't need our coats, so we rolled them into pillows and curled up.

A sharp pain in my side woke me. When I opened my eyes, I saw that we were crouching in a small circle of men. All of them wore uniform. The shiny black boot that had kicked me was now tapping impatiently. Its owner was very tall, and his uniform was stretched tight over his arms and chest, as if it was too small.

"And what might you two lads be doing on the forks-all deck?" said the shiny-boot man.

Without waiting for a reply, he bent over and pressed his face up against mine. "You're really for the high jump now," he whispered. I didn't know what he meant to do to us, but the tone of his voice made me shiver.

He stood up again and looked first at me, then at Jack. "Are you two brothers? Whose bright idea was this?"

Jack opened his mouth to speak, but I was too quick for him. He had been so good to me and I wasn't going to let him take the blame.

"I found the spot—" I blurted out— "and showed Jack how to get here. He knew nothing about the deck before."

"David—" Jack began but he was interrupted by one of the other sailors who was looking at me. "I know this ruffian. 'E's from steerage. 'E's travelling on his own."

"But this one's not," said another. "He's cabin class. We'd better let him go."

The big sailor pushed Jack away. "Run along, you scallywag, before I change my mind."

Jack gave me a look of real panic, but I shook my head. He got the message, and fled.

"I've done nothing wrong!" I said.

The huge sailor with the shiny boots turned

back to me. "Oh, is that so?" He stepped closer and grabbed my collar.

"Let go of me, you great gorilla!"

A strange scowl curled on his lip. "A hairy ape, am I now?" I couldn't tell whether he was angry or amused. "I'll teach you to trespass on this ship," he said.

He dragged me to the engine room and almost threw me inside. I sprawled on the steel floor and heard the door clang shut behind me. The next thing I saw was his enormous fist, held within an inch of my nose. "Nobody calls me a gorilla and gets away wiv it."

The beating he gave me wasn't the worst I've ever had. I've had more of a bruising in the school playground, for he took care not to hit my face. Even so, he knocked me down a couple of times, and I caught my forehead on the iron floor. When it swelled up, the blows stopped, and he half dragged, half marched me back to steerage, and handed me over to the chief steward.

Everyone in the cabin turned to stare at us. I blushed crimson and crept back to my bunk. The children sniggered at my misfortune, and their parents clucked their tongues in disapproval.

I'm writing this on my bunk, lying on my back, because that's the only part of me that isn't sore and throbbing.

Tuesday 2 October

Our capture yesterday has ended my visits to Jack, for the steerage steward makes sure that he *always* knows exactly where I am. His watchful eye makes me feel that the steel walls of our cabin are pressing inwards, trapping me here. It's made worse because I can *see* Jack, but I can't *meet* him. This morning he came and leaned over the rail of the 2nd promenade deck, and we had a shouted conversation, but apart from this we haven't spoken.

As it turns out, this hardly matters, for several curious things happened today that signalled our voyage is nearly over. The crew came down into our cabin with mops and buckets and cleaned the floor and the bathroom. I was baffled by this until I talked to an old man who's made the crossing before.

"It's because we'll be in New York soon," he told me, "and the health people will check the ship. The shipping line don't want them to know that we've been living like dogs for a week."

There have been other changes, too. There was more hot water for washing, and the food is better: I ate ALL THREE meals and threw nothing from the deck rail! We also had a medical inspection. This took hardly half a minute, most of it spent punching seven holes around the outside of my medical ticket. These show that the doctor has checked me on each day of the journey (even though I'd never seen him before this morning).

These signs of our approach made my companions in steerage joyful and excited but also frightened. Everyone has been preparing themselves for the inspections we'll face. Suitcases that have been locked tightly shut have suddenly burst open. Nobody wants to be barred from entering because they look dirty or dowdy. I did just as everybody else did, though my reasons were different. I am *certain* I will be let in, but want to look my best when my uncle and aunt meet me at the docks. When I opened my bag I was unsure what I could put on. Next to Jack's smart clothes that I'd become used to wearing, everything I brought looked tired and worn out.

The excitement has continued until now. Our stuffy cabin, normally filled with snoring by the middle of the evening, echoes with busy chatter. I write this not because there's much to say, but because sleep is impossible.

Wednesday 3 October: America!

This morning a sound like thunder shook the ship. Jerking awake, I glanced towards the porthole I could see from my bunk. Everything looked normal: just a dull grey like any other North Atlantic dawn. As I rubbed my eyes, I realized that the rumbling noise was actually the sound of stamping feet. For the stairs leading to the deck was a mass of struggling, impatient bodies. I seemed to be the only one still in my bunk.

This could mean only one thing

We had reached AMERICA!

I threw on my trousers, doing up only the top button. I dived into a jumper, leaped from my bunk to the floor and threw myself up the companionway two steps at a time.

When I reached the deck I could see even less than through the porthole. The deck rail was crowded three-deep. I had to stand on a winch to see over their shoulders.

It hardly seemed worth the trouble! All I could see was a light in the distance flashing now and then. Everything else was silver sky and grey sea, mixing up together in the middle.

I asked about the flashing and Mr Doherty told

me it was a lighthouse on Nantucket, and that we were still hours away from New York. I shivered. A flashing light seemed a poor reason to get out of a warm bed.

Through the hubbub on the deck I heard a whistle and a shout: "David!"

It was Jack. He was waving from the cabin passengers' promenade deck above. There was too much noise on my deck for him to hear anything I shouted back. I glanced up towards our secret meeting place – just in time to see a pair of crewmen hurry up the stairs that led to it. If I was going to try and meet up with Jack again I would have to find some other place to cross into cabin class.

I looked back up at Jack. He had a pencil in his hand and was scribbling on a piece of paper. Then, suddenly, he looked up and was waving at me. He pulled back his arm and flung something through the air. It curved down towards our deck and I had to jostle the people around me to catch it. It was a bread roll! I inspected it carefully and instantly saw why Jack had thrown it. Pushed into a finger-hole in the bun was a rolled-up piece of paper.

I uncurled it and read:

Meet me in Manhattan.
We are staying at the Imperial
Hotel, on Broadway at 31st St.

I looked up, but Jack was gone.

I stayed on deck another five minutes before the cold drove me back down. When I returned, later in the morning, I caught my first *real* glimpse of America. In the distance, just above the sea and just below the clouds, I saw the very tops of enormous buildings. As we drew gradually closer, so the buildings grew, as if they were coming up out of the water. They were so huge, and so many, and so crowded together that I thought there must be no space at all for people in New York.

I was sitting on my luggage, for a steward had told all of us to get ready for a baggage inspection. Now he unlocked a gate and waved us through onto the cabin class passengers' promenade deck. As we filed up the companionway, there was much excitement at being allowed on this special deck. From time to time cabin passengers had thrown food from it, as if steerage passengers were animals in a zoo. I had walked on this deck many times with Jack, but of course I kept silent about this.

When all of us had lined up, I heard the gate clang shut once more, and we waited ... and waited. Perhaps an hour passed. The engines stopped. We heard the anchor rattle into the water. Still we waited. My teeth chattered. Then I saw a launch approach from far ahead; the crew threw down a line, and several people stepped aboard. The first was dressed in a smart uniform and had an eagle embroidered on his cap. Three or four more followed, one carrying a fat black leather bag.

Several minutes later this group appeared in front of us, and we all began to shuffle back towards steerage. When my turn came the man who'd carried the black bag aboard took my medical certificate, and looked at it for a moment and then back at me. His gaze brought me up in goose pimples. Was he going to return me to Ireland?

It seemed like an age before he nodded to the man with the eagle on his hat. To my huge relief he

pinned a pink piece of cardboard onto my coat.

"Show it off," he said. "It's your ticket to enter America."

As I returned to my luggage, I took a look at my tag. It was printed with the name of the ship and some big numbers, and my name was written on it. Hoorah! Soon I will meet my uncle and aunt and I'll have a real family again!

Thursday 4 October

Yesterday, I thought my journey was over. Now I feel it has hardly begun because it turned out we were still some way off from the city when I wrote my diary.

Our ship steamed closer and closer, and there was a great shout of "Hoorah!" when we passed a gigantic green-grey statue of a woman holding up a torch which marks the *real* entrance to the harbour.

Now, though, fear has taken the place of excitement. Everyone talks about more inspections and questions that new immigrants face before they become Americans. I saw that I'd celebrated too soon. The man who gave me a pink card had lied. There are more tests ahead. I caught the worried mood of the other passengers as if it was a disease.

I'm also worried about my uncle and aunt. Will my uncle be like my da? Will they like me? I wonder whether they live in a big house, or a little one like ours. I don't even know how many cousins I have.

Our ship made the last part of its journey with the help of two tiny steamboats. These were so small that they made me think of two mice towing a horse. They were powerful, though, and pulled our ship right past the tall towers that stretched towards the clouds above New York. I thought we'd tie up in their shadow, but instead the tugs took us to a pier on the *other* side of the river.

There again we waited ... and waited, just as we'd waited for the doctor's inspection yesterday. (In fact, I am beginning to believe that America should really be called the Land of Long Waits.) From the deck rail I watched the first-class passengers go ashore. Many had friends and relatives to greet them. More were driven away in horse cabs – one even in a sleek black motor car.

Then the second-class passengers left the ship. I scanned the gangway to catch sight of Jack and eventually spotted him. From the dockside he turned to look back at the ship. I frantically waved and yelled, but the shouts of the other passengers and the noise of the docks drowned out my voice. Peter tugged at his arm to hurry him along, and he was gone. I wish I could have gone with him.

I reached into my pocket, unfolded the piece of paper he'd thrown me, and read again the name of the hotel where he was staying. I am going to meet him there as soon as I can.

Then it was our turn. From beyond the walls of the wharf we could hear the sound of the city calling us. Indeed, we could even smell it, for the city smells quite different from the sea. We were so close to the new lives that we'd imagined and dreamed of, but we couldn't begin them yet.

We all pushed and shoved to be first down the gangway, but the stewards pushed back harder. When one armed himself with a thick ugly lump of wood studded with nails, the pushing stopped. Eventually, he let us through and we struggled down the gangway to the pier and (as I thought then) to our new home.

But I was wrong *again*. This was just a stopping

point in a voyage that isn't yet over. For after looking at the pink tags on our coats, and chalking mysterious marks on our luggage, the port officials herded us into barges. Before we could complain we were off out across the river once more! I began to weep, for I thought they were returning us to our ship, and by this, to Ireland.

This too was a mistake. We have come somewhere far worse. As I write this, I'm no better off than a prisoner sitting in a jail cell. My prison is a place called Ellis Island, and I don't know when I shall escape, or indeed, if I ever will.

Friday 5 October

The barges that brought us to Ellis Island yesterday tied up at a quay, where a man with the loudest voice I've ever heard shouted at us to line up. The men formed one line, everyone else another. We were bullied and shoved as if we were cattle. They prodded us towards a very grand, tall building that looked like a railway station. It had tall towers at each corner, each one topped with a green dome.

Once inside, those with lots of luggage had to leave it in a store. I was allowed to pass, because I

only had one bag. An official pushed me up a wide flight of stairs to join a queue where a row of men inspected us. They took the health tickets that we'd been given on board our steamer, looked at them closely and stamped them.

They also stopped a few of us and with pieces of blue chalk drew marks on our coats – some got a "C" or an "FT" or a whole alphabet of other letters. I got an "F".

After this I looked at what was happening at the front of the line, and I saw that those with chalk marks were taken aside. A doctor was looking closely at the eyes of a man with an "E" chalk mark. Another, with "L" on his back, was limping, and a doctor had made him take his shoes off. Those without chalk marks walked straight through.

When I got the chance, I took off my coat, and carefully folded it over my arm. I took the tag from my coat and pinned it onto my shirt.

The stairs led into the middle of a vast hall, divided by a metal net and rails into a maze of cages. Now I felt even more like an ox on its way to market. Two doctors looked at me. The first studied my face and body; the second roughly thrust a metal hook against my eyelid and tugged at my eyelashes. When I cried out at the pain, he patted my arm. He told me not to worry, as he'd found nothing to keep me out. With this cheering news, I was sent to wait in a pen for my turn to come. Moments later, to my delight, the whole Doherty family walked in! We were together again because their names and mine are on the same page of the ship's manifest – the book that records every passenger's details.

Together we waited some more. At first we talked, but I soon ran out of things to say. Others in the same pen didn't. They huddled together in little whispering groups. If I leaned forward and listened carefully, I could hear hissed arguments going on: "Tell 'em you have a job to go to and won't be a burden"… "Don't be foolish! Say you have no job!" … "Don't let them know how much money you've got!" … "Tell them you're penniless!" … "Say you have ten dollars!" … "Twenty dollars!" … "Fifty dollars!" Everyone was sure they had the best plan to outwit the inspector and make sure they were admitted.

Our names were called out and, one by one, we left our seats in the cage. I watched those whose names came before mine walk down the hall. At the end an inspector stood behind a tall desk. I strained to catch what he said, mostly without success. I could hear only three words clearly: "Welcome to America!"

I heard this over and over again, and watched the delight spread across the faces of those whose interviews ended this way. But not all did. Some instead were led away, downcast. Where did they go?

It was my turn before the Dohertys. I thought I'd see them moments later, so I didn't even turn to say goodbye. If I'd known what was to follow, I would have hugged and kissed them all farewell.

I walked over to one of the tall desks and stared up at the man behind it. He sucked a pen and stared back.

"Name?" He was Irish, just like me! Surely he'd welcome me to America?

"David O'Connor."

"Age?"

I told him this, too.

"Where did you come from in Ireland?"

I answered this, but then said, "These questions

are just the same as those I answered before coming on board the ship at Queenstown. Why do I need to answer them a second time?"

He sighed impatiently. "Because, lad, I want to see if you give just the same answers. I have to decide whether you are a moron, an idiot, a lunatic, a criminal, or guilty of moral tur-pea-tude."

I didn't know what this last thing meant but from the way he said it I guessed it must be something truly, terribly bad. Then he smiled, leaned forward and stared me straight in the eye.

"So you're going to stay with your uncle and aunt, are you, lad?"

I nodded. He looked back at his form. He scratched his head.

"You're a bit young to be travelling on your own. Where are your mam and da?"

"I'm an orphan."

"Well," he said, "you'll have to wait here until your uncle or aunt comes to collect you. Do they know you're here?"

I answered this question as truthfully as all the others. "I'm sure they do, sir. For Mr Foster wrote to my uncle and told him what ship I would be on."

The inspector scratched his head again.

But as I thought about it I realized that, being

a careful man, Mr Foster wouldn't have wasted money on a telegram, for a letter's cheaper. It would have crossed the Atlantic as I'd done: on a ship. Possibly even on my ship. My uncle and aunt almost certainly didn't know I was here, and might not find out for a week or more. My heart sunk into my boots, and I decided not to say anything about this.

Once more the inspector scratched his head.

"Well, there's nobody waiting for you. We're going to have to keep you here at least until tomorrow."

I began to panic. My life in New York was being snatched away from me. I glanced around the huge room to see if there was anywhere I could run to. Perhaps I could sneak on board a barge and return to the dock we'd come from?

There was nowhere, and anyway, I wasn't quick enough. Dipping his pen in the ink well, the official scratched a note alongside my name and waved his arm. At this, a man standing nearby stepped forward. He led me away up another staircase to a balcony that surrounds the big, bustling hall. I looked down and strained my eyes to see the Dohertys and wave to them. They were the closest thing I had left to a family. I couldn't spot them. Dread and despair filled me up as I left the huge hall behind me.

Saturday 6 October

I hate it here! I feel all at once trapped, lonely, and frightened, for I'm stuck in a nowhere place. Everything about it is "not". I'm NOT on the ocean or in Ireland any more, but I'm NOT yet in America. I'm NOT on a ship, but I'm NOT properly on the land. They tell us that we're NOT prisoners, but we can't go anywhere, so we're NOT free, either.

When I try to think of what this place IS, rather than what it is NOT, I can only think of bad things. The stink. The boredom. The constant sobbing. Most of all the fear. All of us are frightened that we'll be sent back.

In some ways, little has changed since I left the ship. I sleep on a bunk bed that's very like those in steerage. I'm still surrounded by salt water, stopping my escape. In fact, all that's really different from a ship is that now my world doesn't pitch and sway with each breath of wind.

At least the food is better than on the *Campania*. With every meal I get biscuits and milk. For breakfast there is coffee, bread and butter. For dinner, beef stew, potatoes and bread. And we get supper, too. All this is served on *real* plates painted with a picture of Ellis Island and the letters "HB".

Nobody knows what these letters mean, and we all try to guess. When I suggested "Homeward Bound" the crying – which had almost stopped while we ate – began once more.

Crying is the sound of this place. It's there from when I awake to when I lie down at night. I wouldn't sleep if I didn't first blot out the wailing with screws of paper in my ears. In between, there's always someone sobbing: from fear, or homesickness, or just sickness – though the really ill ones are taken to the hospital.

I haven't cried yet, but I think I might if I have to stay here much longer.

There are good reasons to cry. Many of us are parted from our families, because we're living men and boys in one room, and women and girls in another. To make things worse, some here can't speak a word of English. They misunderstand much of what they hear. Worst of all, we're all crowded in, hundreds – perhaps thousands of us – together.

It's worse by day, when our room is a waiting room. To make this possible they do something which I wouldn't have believed if I hadn't seen it with my own eyes. The beds we sleep on are hung from metal chains, and are stacked three high. This is just as on the ship, but here in the early morning we must skip out of our blankets, for men in uniform come round and turn handles that LIFT THE BEDS UP TO THE CEILING! Then more people flood into the room until there is space only to stand up.

Sunday 7 October

I'm sure that when this place was built, they chose the spot just to tease us. For the windows look out towards the tall buildings of New York. The city is so close, yet completely out of reach. Even darkness doesn't hide this tempting view, for it's so *bright*. At home "night" means "darkness". If there's no moon, you might as well have your eyes closed, you can see so little. Here, though, lights twinkle from every window, and huge advertising signs flash in the distance.

I slept barely a wink last night, for – like everyone here – I share a bed with countless insects that tickle and bite us. They run all over the two thin blankets that are all we have for bedclothes. When we arrived we had to strip naked and wash in strange-smelling water that sprayed out of the ceiling like warm rain. While we did this our clothes passed through a machine that was supposed to kill all bugs. In fact, it just ruined our clothing.

I was mistaken about the food. Though there is plenty, the menu is the same each day.

Monday 8 October

Again no word from my uncle, so I'm STILL a prisoner, but something new gives me hope. Each day charity workers come here, and I have caught the eye of an Irish woman who brings food and clothes. She spotted that I'd been here for three days, when most people move on after one or two nights. Perhaps she also saw my downcast look and took pity on me, for she came over and said, "Hey, you've been here a long time, fellah! Where are your folks?"

I told my story to her. By the time I told her about Da dying she was already sniffing. She gave me something to eat. It was like a little strip of grey cardboard, wrapped up in silver paper. She said, "It's candy that you chew," so I put it in my mouth. It tasted like the mint leaves that grow in the marsh. I chewed it and carried on.

When I got to the bit about leaving Pat and

his family on the train, she was saying, "Whoa, a little orphan waif, is it?" and dabbing at her eyes. I stopped for a moment, because the thing she'd given me to chew was very strange. It was rubbery, like eating a cow's stomach. Though it had been sweet at first, now it tasted of nothing at all. No matter how much I chewed it, it didn't get less. In the end I stuck it under my tongue and finished my story. I added a few bits to make it sadder.

I needn't have bothered. She got out a pad and pencil and wrote down my name and my uncle's name and address and promised she'd try and do something for me.

Through the window today I saw a woman with black skin step off one of the ferries! She was not *really* black, though, as I'd heard some people say they are. She was more of a dark brown colour. This made me think about my skin, too. They say I am white, but I'm really more of a pink colour. And by the end of the summer, I've turned brown from the sun. Nothing ever seems to be as people say it is.

Will I be here for ever? Each day is longer than the one before. Because I've nothing better to do I spent an hour rearranging the letters of this dreadful place.

ELLIS ISLAND = LIES AND ILLS.

I saw Mrs Mulligan again, the woman from the aid society, and she hugged me and her voice cracked when she spoke. She promised to help me a second time, but this time I think she really will.

Apparently there's a school for children here sometimes, but I can see no sign of it. Between meals we do as we please. If it's not too crowded or too cold we go on the roof. It's flat and some of us make up teams to kick a football around. It's fine sport while it lasts, even though we all speak different languages. However, the wire mesh that pens in the roof isn't high enough, and the third time the ball went over it we lost it.

I'm told there are even motion-picture shows, but how can this be true? There isn't a picture house in the whole of Ireland. If all the free people of Ireland cannot watch motion pictures, why should the prisoners of Ellis Island be better off?

Today there were fights in the waiting room. I shrank into a corner when they started, and made myself as small as I could, in case someone picked on me. A ship has brought families from Romania, and many of the children are sick. When the doctors took them to the hospital, a rumour spread that they'd sent them away to be cooked and eaten. Their parents can speak no English and now they attack any official or doctor who dares come through the door.

Wednesday 10 October

At last! Mrs Mulligan came today and took me down to the telegraph office here, so that I could send a message to my uncle. The cost of the message was more than I had, for the money the Fosters had given me was all gone. However, Mrs Mulligan loaned me the money. The telegraph office would allow me only ten words, so I wrote on the form:

```
YOUR ORPHAN NEPHEW DAVID O'CONNOR AWAITS
       ELLIS ISLAND. PLEASE COME.
```

When I'd sent it, Mrs Mulligan said to me, "Steady on! If you smile any wider than that, your face will crack in two!" which I suppose she thought was funny.

The Romanian men are calm now. When they grew hungry enough they had to talk to someone. A translator persuaded some of them to go to the hospital, where they saw their children. They were not eaten, and doctors and nurses were caring for them.

Thursday 11 October: freedom!

At three o'clock this afternoon my aunt Mary arrived here at Ellis Island and signed the papers to release me. I was so relieved that I ran up to her and gave her a huge hug, even though we'd never met before. She seemed rather taken aback. She took my hand, then with her other one she pulled an envelope from her bag, and said, "Here, this is for you. It came in the same post as the letter from – what's 'e called? – Mr Forester?

I recognized Pat's handwriting. I tore open the envelope so fast that I nearly ripped the letter in half. He always had trouble with writing at school, so I wasn't surprised it was short.

DEAR DAVID,

   I HOPE YOU HAVE ARRIVED SAFELY IN AMERICA. I REALLY MISS YOU HERE, THOUGH THERE IS MORE SPACE IN MY BEDROOM NOW.

   NOT A LOT HAS HAPPENED. THE GARDA CAME TO THE SCHOOL THIS WEEK AND TALKED TO US ALL. THEY SAID THERE WERE SOME CHILDREN'S FOOTPRINTS BY THE LAKE. I TOLD THEM WE WENT THERE TO LOOK AT BIRDS. THEY NODDED AND SAID, "YES, THERE ARE LOTS, ARE THERE NOT?"

   THEN THE GARDA OFFICER PUT HIS HAND ON MY SHOULDER AND HELD IT TIGHT AND SAID, "YOU ARE TELLING THE TRUTH, ARE YOU NOT?" SO I SAID, "YES, OFFICER." AND THEN HE SAID, "IS THERE ANYTHING ELSE YOU ARE NOT TELLING ME?" IN A WAY THAT SCARED ME.

   REMEMBER WHAT I SAID AT THE STATION.

   WRITE SOON TO TELL ME WHAT YOU ARE DOING.

                              YOUR FRIEND,

                                   PATRICK

When my aunt gave me the letter, I couldn't wait to read it. Now I wished I'd never opened it. All the fear that I had felt before I left our town came rushing back. I felt like the terror was going to drown me. I imagined the garda coming to Pat's house at dawn, and of steel doors clanging shut behind him.

As I folded up the letter and put it in my pocket, I realized my aunt was talking to me. She was saying, "David, David?" over and over. When I looked up, she added, "What's the matter with you? You look like you've seen a ghost." Then she asked suddenly, "What became of the money from Sean's farm? I thought he bought it three years past."

I told her about the farm and the debts, and Da's illness and sudden death. And about my journey across the sea, and Ellis Island. And when I'd finished, she said, "You talk a lot, don't you?"

She pulled me roughly towards the ferry terminal, telling me, "Never mind about the cost of the telegram. You'll soon earn it."

On the ferry to the other side of the harbour I asked her where my uncle Dermott was and when would I see him. Her first answer was to cuff me round the ear, and then she sobbed out a stream of curses and sorrowful cries in Irish and American. "He's in jail!" she said finally. "In jail for being a GOOD MAN!"

Then she told me his sad story. Until a month ago my uncle had a workshop making horse harnesses, and the family lived in a modest apartment in a good neighbourhood. But motor cars are rapidly taking over from carts ("They're *shooting* the horses," she added with disgust), so the business was not doing as well. With less money, my uncle could no longer pay the men who protected his factory from damage, and one night it caught fire. My uncle found out it was one of these men who'd *started* the fire! He went to the police, but because he couldn't pay them a bribe, they arrested HIM for starting the fire himself. "Within a week," she sobbed, "we were thrown out of the house. And now I'm left alone with no money, two children, and now *you*!"

Pat's letter, and the one his da had written warning of my arrival had gone to the old address. They would have been lost, if a neighbour hadn't seen the telegraph boy trying to deliver the telegram I sent from Ellis Island. She sent the boy to the correct house and gave him the two letters to take as well.

By this time we'd reached the ferry terminal, and stepped into New York itself. There I saw with my own eyes the most astonishing thing: a railway line *in the sky*. At first I couldn't believe it, but the horrible grinding, shrieking and rattling sound of its wheels told me that this *really was* a railway. I looked down at the street below to see whether other people found it as alarming as I did. To my surprise they paid it no mind at all. Even horses ignored the huge trains.

Seeing my open-mouthed astonishment, my aunt tugged again at my hand, saying, "Come along,

David. We can't afford to take the Hell. We can walk a few blocks."

I'd thought that the fine, tall buildings I'd seen from the ship would cover all of New York, but I quickly learned that I was mistaken. The streets through which my aunt led me are low in every way. They are darker, dirtier and more dismal than anything I've seen before.

They are filled with constant, noisy traffic that never seems to stop. On the buildings that face the street, there's hardly a single brick that isn't covered in words. Signs painted right on the wall advertise medicines that can cure *anything*. They shout the names and skills of opticians, photographers, grocers, undertakers – every trade you can imagine and some I haven't heard of. Then there are enamel and wooden signs fighting for attention. And finally, near the ground, countless posters, still wet with glue, encouraging passers by to talk with the dead at a spiritualist meeting, or to see a man eat swords and broken glass.

Each time I stopped to read one of these I fell further behind my aunt. My bag was a burden, too, and its weight must surely have stretched my arms, for sometimes it dragged on the ground.

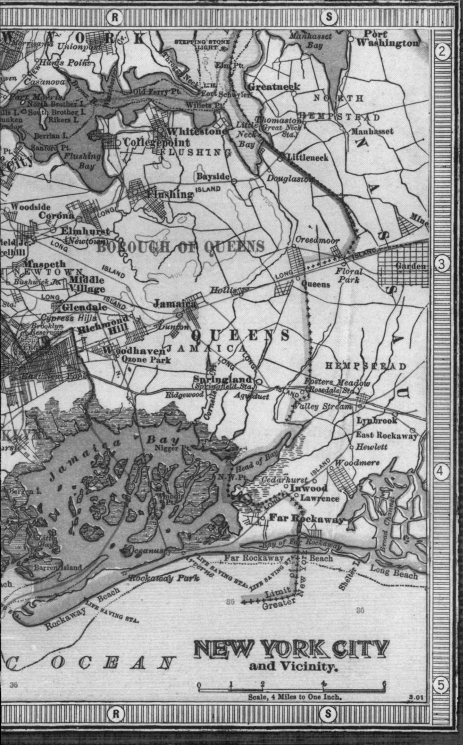

At times my aunt had to halt while I caught up, and then she chided me for my slowness.

Finally she said, "Here we are!"

I looked up at what seemed like a fine (if paint-peeled) house of four storeys. But when I turned round my aunt was gone. I was baffled until I noticed a narrow alleyway at the side of the building. Glancing down it, I saw her rapidly disappearing at the far end. I followed her … and came out into a tiny courtyard. Chickens scratched in the mud and a goat was tied up in a corner. It was far more bony and tatty than any beast we ever kept on the farm. There was a stink like blocked drains. The yard had once been much bigger, but now almost all the space is taken up with a tall, rambling wooden building. It rises higher than the house on the street, yet is hidden behind it.

We climbed rickety stairs to the sixth floor. My aunt drew a key from her pocket and let us in.

When I stepped through the door I couldn't see anything at first. Though it was still day, little light or air finds its way into the room. There's just one window. Its glass is cracked and filthy but just in case this should fail to keep out the sun, there are curtains. Once they might have been lace. Now they are rags.

From the corner of my eye I could see something moving in the shadows. I turned and saw a bed. It seemed to have coats instead of blankets, and from beneath them smiled two faces.

"Who're you?" said one grin.

Before I could answer, my aunt said, "Michael, find your cousin some bread. He's come all the way from Ireland." Except that she said, "Eye-ur-land."

A young boy climbed slowly from the bed, scratching himself all over. He cut me the thinnest slice of bread I've ever seen from a stale loaf on the table, and poured water from a jug into a chipped enamel mug. As he passed his mother he hurried, holding up one hand to cover the ear nearest her.

My aunt pointed at the bed. "You'll have to sleep with these two. We don't have much room here, but at least you'll be warm: warmer with three than two, eh, Michael?"

Michael nodded silently but didn't smile.

I ate the bread and drank the water without taking off my coat, for it was cold and there was no fire in the grate.

"Is there no turf to light a fire?" I asked. Only my aunt knew what I was talking about. She replied sharply, "You might make yourself useful by picking up some firewood at the market. They throw away crates and boxes there."

And this I did. For the damp cold of the building (which is called a "tenement") chilled me to the bone. I was glad to go outside again.

I'm writing this by the light of the fire, but it's dying so low that there's hardly enough light to see any more, and my pencil grows blunt.

My new life in America is not at all what I'd expected or hoped for. This is a dismal place. Worse than that, it's the meanest, dirtiest, most horrible place I've ever stayed. It's called "Cherry Street", which makes it sound like an orchard or something pleasant. But if there were ever cherry trees here, they were chopped down for firewood long ago.

My aunt is not like my mam, or Mrs Foster. She is not even like an aunt, but more like someone who doesn't know me or like me. My cousins are no better. They are sly and quick and seem to like me no more than their mother. I will have to stay here, but I don't feel welcome.

Thursday 18 October

It's hard not to compare this place with home. Though Da and I had no money, there was nothing

we wanted. Fuel for the fire, we dug up from the bog. Our bony cows gave us fresh milk. Our hens laid four eggs a day. We breathed fresh air and there was clear water in the well.

In these crowded rooms there are none of these to be had, not even air. Nobody eats unless they earn their crust. (In fact, crusts are all that keep us from dying here.) Instead of going to school, I now find ways to earn a few coins to bring home to my aunt. There are, surprisingly, many ways for a boy like me to do this. Some younger than me have proper jobs. A few carry brushes and tins of polish, and make money blacking shoes. Young ones sell newspapers. When I asked Michael how he made a living, he reeled off a long list.

"You can sell stuff: I've sold sweet potatoes, baked pears, hot corn, string, pins. You can easily find stuff to sell, like bits of firewood, rags, rope, nails, bottles – you get a dime a dozen for them – bones, grease, coal and metal. You can sell them all. Then there's stuff that people throw out. Rotting meat – you cut off the smelliest bits and sell the rest at the back door of a restaurant. Down on the docks a knife makes sure stuff spills out of sacks as they unload it, and you can fill a bag with spilled sugar, or coffee or flour. And stuff comes off houses: lead from the roof if you can get up there, drain pipes, brass doorknobs – someone will pay you for all of them. Last summer I caught butterflies and sold them to a man to feed to his canaries. But that was before we were poor."

I'm learning quickly that he's right. Today I made a few coins holding the reins of a man's horse while he ran an errand. I made a few more by watching a motor car. I'd seen other boys encourage motorists to pay them by lurking near the kerb with a half-brick. I did this and found a parking driver keen for my "protection".

There's also fetching and carrying – especially beer. For it's a long way from our rooms down to the beer shop and back. I can make a bit by taking a jug (which they call a "growler") down to the saloon, to have it filled, then returning up seventy-eight stairs without spilling a drop.

When I bring back some coins, I can eat. Usually there's bread and a little milk. This looks just like ordinary milk, except that tiny black specks float in it and sometimes straw. It also tastes different – at best thin and watery, but often almost sour. When I've had no luck, I must beg for food, or find it where I can.

Our two rooms here are home not just to our family, but to no less than *two* others. Not to mention a hundred families of rats and mice, and a thousand of fleas and lice. The vermin never go out, but usually some of the human occupants are elsewhere, whatever the time of day or night. When we are all here together it's so crowded that I must sleep on the landing. As the last one to arrive, I get the least respect.

A week has gone by since I last kept up my journal, because I'm mocked for writing! When a boy here found my diary he tossed it to one of his brothers. When I ran to catch it, the brother tossed it back, and on to another. But to my relief, none of them can read a word, so they soon lost interest in it! Some of them haven't had a day's schooling in their lives, nor want any. They are proud of knowing nothing and even compete with each other to show who has the least learning.

Now I carry my diary everywhere, hidden under my clothes. To keep it dry I have wrapped it in layers of paper, and a piece of oilcloth that I rescued from a rubbish bin. I feel like a villain or a spy, hiding it like this. Will I ever get out of here?

Saturday 20 October

Yesterday I had a stroke of amazing good fortune.

A well-dressed gentleman was climbing from a hansom. As he reached up over the horse to pay the driver, a dollar bill fluttered from the roll in his hands and fell into a puddle, where the horse stepped on it. The driver didn't notice, and whipped his horse away. Nor did his passenger, who was ten yards down the street when I picked up the money and dried the note on my clothes. There seemed to be no harm in profiting from carelessness. If I didn't scoop up the note then the next passer-by would take it instead.

I told nobody at Cherry Street of this. And today I headed for Park Row, where all the newspapers have their offices. I bought a hundred *Journal*s, thinking that I could just find a corner and sell them. I even had enough left over to buy a stamp, so that I could write to Pat. I'm worried about him, and feel guilty, too. I may be miserable here, but at least I'm safe from the garda.

I did well to begin with, selling a quarter of what I'd bought in just an hour or so. But then another newsboy who was selling nearby spotted me. He came over and challenged me, shouting, "Hey! This is my spot! Get going!"

When I ignored him, he charged at me with his fists raised, but he was so much smaller that I'd no

trouble fending off his blows. Eventually, he gave
up, picking up his papers and running off.

Against what happened next I had no defence.
Within a few minutes he returned with five others.
Before I could flee, they were all over me, kicking,
scratching and biting as well as using their fists. I fell
to the ground, and before I knew it, my papers and
money were gone. When I picked myself up, I was
relieved to find that I'd suffered nothing worse than
a black eye and a few bruises. But I was miserable.

When I returned to Cherry Street I couldn't hide my injuries, and I told my aunt about my setback. The lost money drove her into a fury.

"I would have spent it wisely, and you squandered it, you waster!" she screamed.

She picked up a pan, and would have added to my wounds if I hadn't run away down the stairs. Even her sons shrank from her temper, and they're used to it. They didn't care about my lost fortune and seemed more excited by my swollen face. Calling my eye a "shiner", they seemed to think of the bruise as a kind of medal, as if it made me more like them.

When we judged that it was safe to go back into the apartment, my aunt was at the sink. She didn't turn round, but told me she'd found me a "less dangerous job" to do tomorrow. I didn't dare ask what it's to be.

Sunday 21 October

My "safe work" turned out to be making paper violets for ladies' hats. "We can earn good money—" my aunt told me— "if we get our fingers nimble and quick." And she sat me down at the table to watch her make the flowers.

She took petals from one pile, and stems from another, dipping the stems deftly in a pot of glue. She slipped the petals up the stem, quickly squeezed with her fingertips, and laid the finished flower on a pile.

I make this sound simple, but her fingers moved so swiftly that they blurred before my eyes.

"There," she said, waving to a growing pile of paper blooms. "Now you try. Twelve dozen flowers pays us ten cents. If the four of us work at it, we can make a dollar a day."

So we set to work. But as fast as I dipped stems in glue, my aunt snatched them from me and made flowers. I was never quick enough. By noon my hands were numb and my arms ached. My aunt just said, "There's a knack, you'll soon learn." But this made the work no easier.

Tuesday 23 October

My aunt set me doing flowers again yesterday morning, but I fell so far behind that I carried on at it long after darkness had fallen. My head kept lolling forward, until I felt a sudden heat, and the room was full of shouting. I had dozed off and knocked over stacked boxes of completed flowers.

One tumbled into the gaslight and the whole table of scattered petals was aflame.

Fortunately one of my aunt's man-friends, who I must call "uncle", saw the fire and rushed in. He used a growler of beer (which is for ever at hand) to douse the flames.

Shocked and still drowsy, I gasped at him, "You saved our lives!" But when I glanced around the wrecked and smoking room, I quickly guessed what was coming, for we'd lost all of our afternoon's work. His angry face filled me with terror, and I began stammering that it wasn't my fault. I sprung from my seat and darted round the room, looking for somewhere to hide. Finding nowhere safe, I ran for the door. He stood in my path, and I couldn't avoid a thrashing.

This wasn't the last of the beating. The next night I was stretched out in a corner under my coat when a kick woke me. A gentleman caller stumbled over me and fell full length on the floor, smashing the full growler he was carrying. He blamed me for this and sent me to fetch more beer. He gave me no money, telling me I was to "beg, borrow or steal" the money and find a new pitcher.

I'd rather have died than do this, so I fled the house and slept (or rather, passed the night) under a bridge.

This morning I watched the house until I saw the man leave with my aunt, then slunk back. I meant to take all my belongings, and I worried that I mightn't be able to carry them far.

I needn't have worried. Most of the clothes I owned had gone: stolen, I guess, or sold to pay for beer. Fortunately, my thick jacket was still there.

I grabbed it, then rushed to pick up everything else I could find. I was nervous. The apartment was empty, but this was very unusual, and someone might return at any time. Every creak on the stairs outside made me jump out of my skin.

I felt in my jacket pockets, and found the slip of paper on which Jack had written the address of his hotel. Thank goodness that hadn't gone.

There was something new in the pocket, too: an envelope, with an Irish stamp and Pat's handwriting! It had been sent to my aunt's old address two streets away, so she must have been collecting letters from there.

My heart was racing as I started to tear the letter open, but then, glancing around, I decided that gathering my property and escaping was more urgent. I packed the jacket and everything else that was left in a small bag, and put on as many clothes as I could find (not just my own, but anything that fitted). I had carefully stitched my father's watch into the lining of my coat to keep safe, so I already had this with me. And I took my box of pencils.

When I was safely away from Cherry Street, I opened Pat's letter and crouched in a doorway to read it.

Dear David,

What's happened to you? I hope you are well. You haven't written to me yet.

We are all good. It is wet here. Ma and Dad and Sue and Mary send their love. The shop is doing a little better now, you will be glad to hear.

There is more good news. The garda arrested an old tinker for the crime of killing the waterman. He is a Catholic, like you. You may remember seeing him here. He smelled and pushed around a rusty old bike with no tyres, loaded with bags of clothes.

Dad says they will not hang him for he is a halfwit and they will just lock him up for a long time.

Your friend,

Patrick

On reading this I let out a great sigh. Not knowing whether Pat was safe had been pressing down on me. It had been like carrying home a great load of turf on my back. I carefully folded up the letter so that I could read it again and reply.

I did all this to the sound of my stomach rumbling loud enough to hear. I'd left Cherry Street hungry, and I hadn't even a cent in my pocket. I wandered down to the East River piers hoping to beg some food from a ship. But before I could reach the water I was surrounded by a gang of lads my age or younger.

"Who do you think you are?" the oldest asked me.

I told him my name, "David O'Connor."

Then, in a threatening way, he asked me, "Do you know where you are?"

Looking up, I read the sign above his head. "Why, yes—" I said— "I'm on the pier of the Standard Fruit and Steamship Company."

To my great relief this made them all laugh, for I'd answered a question he hadn't asked.

"You're a real greenhorn, aincha?" said the biggest. "This is the East River Rats' drag, and you shouldn't be here." He looked me up and down and grinned. "But we'll let you stay, seeing as how you look like you can do with all the help you can get, and you're obviously just off the boat." And with this he clapped me round the shoulders and offered me a cigarette.

"Read that sign there!" a smaller lad shouted, pointing to a safety notice on the wall. I started to read it to him, but before I got more than two sentences in, he yelled, "You're a real little professor, aincha?" and again they all laughed.

So to my new friends I am "the Professor" or just "Prof". They're helping me out of pity, but mostly because they can laugh at my ignorance of the dangers of the street, and how to survive on it. When I tell them that I can snare and skin a rabbit, they laugh even more, and point the way to the Coney Island ferry, for they call rabbits "conies" here. They delight in teaching me the best places to roll a sleeping drunk for his money; which restaurant kitchen throws out the best scraps; and where to sleep in comfort. Some of them spend the night *inside* the girders of a huge bridge. Last night I curled up with two others to sleep warm and dry inside a huge money safe.

To keep out the winter's cold, I put on as many clothes as I could, with my thick coat on top. When I thrust my hands in the pockets to keep them warm, I felt Jack's note. I curled my fingers around it and remembered what fun we had on the ship. I *must* try and get to his hotel soon.

I am useless at "finding" things of value, and even at selling papers, so my new friends employ me to do things that *anybody* can do, or tasks that *none* of them can. When they're afraid that they might be caught thieving from a market stall, they post me as a watchman. This lowly work is usually the job of a much younger boy.

In the second class of tasks is reading and writing. After I joined them yesterday they watched me write a letter to Pat. I covered a sheet of paper from my pad with news for Pat, ending it by telling him that I'd keep our secret until I died.

Then (having no envelope) I carefully folded the paper up and tucked in the flap before addressing it and sticking on the stamp I'd saved.

All of this impressed my new friends, and those who have no work asked me to write begging signs for them. With their help I refined an all-purpose begging letter. This reads "HELP ME" (written bigger than the rest) "hungery, cold and homeles.

HELP ME
hungery, cold and homeles. PLEASE spare a few copers for a meel.

Please spare a few copers for a meel." I am careful with my misspelling, for a correct message brings few donations and more sharp words. The people of New York believe that properly educated boys shouldn't beg.

Monday 29 October

I was so hungry today that (I am ashamed to admit) I stole an apple from a market stall. I was surprised at how easy it was, *and* how little regret I felt afterwards. Perhaps stealing apples is easier because I was accustomed to scrumping in the orchards at home.

Living rough like this has worn me down, and the weather has grown colder. So I decided to return to my aunt and beg her to take me in again. I spent most of the night walking around to keep warm, and at dawn I returned to Cherry Street.

As soon as I rounded the corner, I saw faces I knew. All of the people from the seven floors of the tenement where I lived were hurrying away from it. As I drew closer I saw why. There were two red pumping engines outside. Steam puffed from their chimneys, and rose from the horses that had pulled them. The horses drank from water that flowed down the gutter, though it was speckled with small pieces of charcoal. Closer to the house my nose caught the bitter smell of cold, wet wood ash.

A crowd stood in the street, looking down our alley to where – until a few hours before – my aunt's home had stood. Now there were just soaked, smoking timbers. I stopped all the people I recognized to ask if they had seen my aunt and cousins. They shook their heads. They told me the fire had started in the basement, where a cigarette set light to paint stored there. The fire took hold in seconds, for the whole house was built of cheap timber. The fire escape was blocked with everyone's belongings, and my aunt and cousins didn't manage to flee across the roof to the building next door.

So I am *twice* orphaned. Once again I own nothing more than I carry, and now I have nowhere at all that I can call home. I never thought I'd be brought this low, and I feel ready to sob. All that stops me is the knowledge that it would do me no good at all, and wouldn't fill my empty stomach. My only comfort is that, coming away from the ashes of Cherry Street, I had the good fortune to make friends with some rag-pickers. At least I'm writing this in the warm, dry softness of a great bale of rags, where they'll let me sleep for one night.

Tuesday 30 October

I've had both a disaster and a miraculous piece of good fortune. While I was sleeping in the bale of rags outside a shop, my boots were stolen! I still cannot believe that I didn't awake as they were being unlaced and slipped off. When cold air on my feet woke me the street was silent and deserted.

I managed to wrap my feet in rags and at dawn hobbled in search of something to eat. I'd been begging for change for half an hour, and had collected only a dime, when a well-dressed gentleman hesitated, but then passed on. Guessing that his heart might soften, I put on my most pitiful snivelling voice. I called to him loudly that my boots had been stolen. He turned back and put his hand in his pocket. Just as he did so, a policeman spied what I was up to, and began to cross the street. I was about to bolt away, but the gentleman closed his hand around my arm and told the policeman, "He's with me, officer." I noticed that the cop winked at him before walking away.

After I'd thanked him for this kindness the

gentleman said to me, "I can tell by your accent that you're not long off the boat, are you? Come along with me, lad, and we'll find you some shoes and a meal."

I know I shouldn't have gone. The boys at Cherry Street have told me terrible things about strangers in the city. They lure away plumper children to make into the pies that are sold in cheap restaurants. Michael (I wonder if *he* escaped the fire?) swears this is true because he once found a toe nail in a pie. But I was so very hungry and cold, and the man spoke like an Irishman, and as he did so he let go of my arm, instead of gripping it tighter. This (and the fact that there is little meat left on my bones) made me feel I was safe.

So I went with him. And now here I sit in his fine house, writing my journal. I've had the first good meal since I left Ellis Island. I have on a pair of shoes that pinch a little, but they've no holes. Tonight I have a real bed to sleep in. It's only a folding bed in a servant's room, it's true, but it's warm and soft and has clean blankets. I really feel that my life in America has taken a turn for the better.

I crossed out the sentence above because I've been cruelly tricked. I am learning quickly – but not quickly enough – that nothing in this city is ever what it seems. Only fools trust the kindness of strangers. This is a hard lesson, but it's better perhaps that I learn it now than later, when I've more to lose.

The gentleman that stopped to help me was nothing of the sort. He turns out to be a villain in smart clothes, and I am again a prisoner. For I am *locked up* in this fine town house that I thought was to be my home. Although I've been cold and hungry for the last week, I've also been freer than I ever was before. I could do exactly as I pleased and nobody cared. Now, I can do nothing.

I began to guess my fate as soon as I awoke this morning. Through the closed door I could hear the villain who brought me here talking. At least, his voice sounded like the same person's, but also somehow different. Last night it was as smooth as silk and dripping with kindness. But this morning it was rough and sharp and his words made me fear what he might have planned.

"Tell Mike I've got just the boy he needs for the green goods game in Hell's Kitchen…" I heard him say. "This one's really smart – even knows his letters – but a complete greenhorn."

Then I heard another man talking, this time in the rough accent of those born in this city. "Fresh off the boat is he? Mike needs one like that to sucker in a mark or two!" And they both laughed loudly.

Then a key turned in the door of my room and I heard the house door slam a moment later. Now all I can do is sit here and await my fate.

Thursday 1 November

This morning, I made the most terrifying journey of my life.

My companion on this trip was the man I heard talking in the hall yesterday. He introduced himself as Seamus. He looks nothing like as rough as his speech. He's well-dressed, and wears a flower in his buttonhole, but he scares me. Before we set off, he pressed his face close to mine and warned me.

"Don't try any funny business, because wherever you run to, sonny Jim, I will find you." Then he added for good measure, "Have you heard the stories about children being made into pies?"

I nodded.

"Believe me, they're all true, and I can take you to the kitchen and show you the mincing machine."

I guessed that this was "Hell's kitchen" that I'd heard him talking about yesterday. So I did just as I was told, and followed him out of the house. The street was crowded and I could have tried to escape, but I couldn't forget the mincing machine. I didn't dare run, or ask a passer-by for help.

We reached some wide steps, and he led me down them into a dark tunnel. Now I began to be *really* frightened. People pressed in around me and it got warmer. I heard a heavy rumbling sound. The air in the tunnel started to rush past my face. At that moment I really thought we were going to Hell itself!

I began to pray silently. I truly believed death was only moments away. I would spend for ever in pain and torture, just as Father Joseph warned us in church. The rumbling grew louder and louder, turning into the worst screaming, clattering noise I had ever heard. Then I saw it...!

It was olive green and had a light shining from the front. I can't describe how relieved I was to see that it was just a train.

We climbed on board, and rode as far as a stop called Fiftieth Street. Coming up from the station, we walked a little way, then turned into West Forty-second Street.

At first it was quite smart. There were fine new shops with big, bright windows. The houses were cleaner than on Cherry Street. The neighbourhood soon began to change, though. There were fewer motor cars. The big shop windows disappeared. Gaudy signs half blocked the pavement promising the "Cheapest Suits in Town" and "Kwality Fruits and Vegetabels".

The street got still shabbier and dirtier. There were more boarded-up and wrecked buildings. There were more grimy bars.

After we passed yet another wide avenue, ragged, snot-smeared children crowded in on us, begging for change or cigarettes. They shouted and spat at us when we refused. A revolting stench greeted us on one corner, and I soon saw the source. Rather, I *heard* it, as we walked past a gate: the sad lowing of a frightened beast.

The mooing stopped suddenly and I heard hooves sliding on cobbles. When we'd walked on, I looked back to see two hungry dogs lapping at the bright red, steaming stream that flowed from under the gate.

Adding to the smell were ponds of filth in the

gutter, mountains of rubbish on the pavement, and the greasy stench of factories, breweries, coal yards and oil tanks.

At the next road we crossed we had to wait while a goods train passed by. It clattered RIGHT DOWN THE MIDDLE OF THE ROAD! Beyond and within sight of the river, we ducked through a filthy doorway. I blinked because I couldn't see anything in the darkness, but my companion pushed me onwards and down stone steps into a dank basement. Once inside, I heard a bolt slide behind me.

And it's here, on a pile of orange crates, that I write this. I'm locked in again, waiting to see what the future holds. I wonder where Jack is now? I must be nearer to his hotel than before. If he's left New York, I will – somehow – find the money for my train fare and follow him. I think he's my only hope.

Saturday 3 November

I'm kept a prisoner by a small army of children! They're no more than half my size, but they swagger about as if they own the run-down cellar that is my jail.

None of them use ordinary names, like David O'Connor. Instead they have nicknames. The stranger or crazier these are, the better they like them: Skinny, Crutch Irish, Chalky, Mutton-Head Mo, Fat Billy, Boggy Boy, Scratch, Hinkey, Yellow, English, Pie Face, Red Bull, Blobs, Squeezy, Dopey, Stingey, Spikey and Roper.

I'm free to do as I please here – as long as it pleases them, too. When it doesn't, one of them just stands in my way. If I try to push past, another jumps up to join him. If I still try, a bigger boy comes and threatens to black my eye if I carry on.

It's clear that they've been told to guard me with their lives, but they're all friendly and cheerful. They share their food with me and offer me beer and cigarettes. One introduced me to his moll. She dresses and wears make-up as prettily as any grown-up woman, though she's no more than twelve. Encouraged by his smile, I suggested that I could teach him his letters. He laughed, telling me he doesn't need to read and write for the line of work he's in.

I've also found that my guards don't care a farthing for what I do or say. Nor do they care what I think of them. I'm no more to them than an annoying fly they might swat for disturbing their sleep. This made me bold and I began to question my jailers.

I asked where I'd been taken, and they replied, "Why, to Hell's Kitchen, of course!"

When I tried to find out where this place is, they began arguing. Eventually they decided that Hell's Kitchen is the twenty blocks above Thirty-fifth Street, from Eighth Avenue to the river. Its name has nothing to do with kitchens or meat pies. It was named after a gang called "Hell's Brood", who had a den three blocks south of here.

My next question, about their parents, brought peals of laughter. They told me they've no mams and das, or their parents are drunks, or smoke opium, or have just "gone away". They all live by thieving, but didn't understand when I asked if they were afraid of the garda. When they realized I meant the police, they laughed all the more.

"Nah," said one, "the cops are afraid to come here." He pointed out at a rooftop. "Up there's a pile of bricks and planks. If the cops come we hurl 'em down on their heads." He grinned. "They soon go home."

This caused yet more laughter, but it came to a sudden stop when I asked, "Who's your chief?"

There was a moment's pause, with shuffling feet and scratching the only sounds.

"Mike. He's our boss. One-Eyed Mike. You'll

meet him soon enough. When he judges it's time."

And with this, my jailers lit cigarettes, drifted away upstairs, played cards or talked in pairs or threes.

I want to know what Mike is like. Is he like Seamus? Or like the sailor who beat me on the ship? I'm not sure I want to meet him.

Sunday 4 November

"The right time" came quickly: today I met One-Eyed Mike.

His "office" is the back room of a saloon on Sixty-fifth Street. The young guards who took me there lost their cheeky chumminess when they stepped inside. They spoke to Mike as I used to speak to Mr Birch at school. Mike sent them all away with a silent scowl. He pointed to a chair, and I sat down.

Mike's shoulders are so wide that he has to turn sideways to step through doorways. His hair is quite white, and he has a pale scar that starts at his right ear, crosses his neck and disappears down his shirt front.

Mike brought another chair and sat facing me.

Our knees were almost touching. His eyes met mine – or at least, the left one did. His other he kept closed most of the time. When his right eyelid lifted a little, I glimpsed an eye that was just like its brother – except that it always pointed straight ahead and wasn't bloodshot. It made me shiver. I could see why the others were scared of him.

For what must have been a minute, Mike said nothing. Sitting there, just hearing him breathing an inch from my face, I became more and more nervous.

Finally, he asked me my name, and how I came to be living in Hell's Kitchen. I told him everything, and he said how sad, but I could tell he didn't mean it.

I was glad when he stood up from his chair and walked over to a desk in the corner to fetch a pencil and a piece of paper. The room seemed suddenly brighter, and I realized it was because his great body had been blocking the light from the window.

"I can tell that you are a smart God-fearing lad," he said. "Now write down the Lord's Prayer for me, for I'm sure you know that."

By now I was so terrified that however much I tried, I couldn't bring myself to remember the words, though I say them every day! Afraid to write nothing at all, I scribbled the first thing that came into my head, which was the names of the railway stations I had passed on my way to Dublin.

Mike stopped me before I finished, and held out his hand. Mine was shaking as he took the paper from me. Squinting at it with his one good eye, he said, "Excellent. We shall get along nicely if you do just as you're told." And then he explained what he wanted of me.

Before I can be trusted with the "great task" he has in mind, I must first prove that I'm a "proper codger". I didn't understand what he meant by this, or by much else that he said. If I'm a proper codger, he told me, I will be well rewarded. "But should you prove to be a rat ..." he said and silently drew the edge of his hand across his throat.

I hid my fear behind a question. "What is the 'green goods game', please, sir?"

"Why!" he gasped, with a look of genuine surprise. "Where on earth did you hear that?" He lifted his enormous boot and kicked my chair from under me, sending me sprawling on the dirty floor. As I picked myself up, he shouted, "Sly! Get in here!"

The door opened, and I found myself staring up at the grinning face of the man who brought me to Hell's Kitchen.

"David, Sly Seamus will make sure that you get home without being knocked down crossing the road." And with a nod, he sent us on our way.

Tuesday 6 November

Last night I was set to work by my new family (for this is how I've come to think of the mob that I've been forced to join). The target of our efforts was an express wagon making deliveries in the neighbourhood. At first I was scared of getting caught, but One-Eyed Mike's ugly face pressed close to mine made it clear to me that I had no alternative.

Four of us went a few blocks away and waited in the street for a wagon from Dodd's, or the US Express. I hid with Scratch and Mutton-Head Mo, while Spikey stood at a corner. Just as the wagon drew close, he ran across the road, and pretended to trip on a cobble. The driver hauled back on the reins and brought his wagon to a halt with Spikey almost beneath the wheels. As he cursed Spikey, we ran from our hiding place and leaped lightly on the back of the wagon. When it set off again and the rattle of the wheels hid the noise we made, we began throwing packages from the wagon. Spikey followed behind, picking up everything he could.

This we did until the driver noticed what we were up to. He pulled on the reins and turned to grab us. Now my fear of capture turned to terror. I froze as if the winter's cold had turned me to ice. But just as the driver advanced towards me, Mutton-Head Mo grabbed me and hurled me into the street.

The four of us fled, and in moments we were away into the dark shadows of the alleys.

I know I should feel bad about joining in on this scheme, but I don't. To everyone around me, this is what they call their work. They think nothing of it. Indeed, they're proud of what they do. Last night's game raised two hundred and fifty dollars, locked in a leather satchel, which we cut open. For my work I received but a dollar, because I played the least part in it, and was learning the trade. I shall spend some of it on a stamp to write to Pat; perhaps a little on food. But I shall save most of it for my train fare in case Jack has already left New York and I have to follow him out West.

Keeping this journal has become difficult, because the gang is suspicious of my writing: Hinkey once caught me with the pencil and journal and asked me what I was up to. I grabbed a newspaper off the floor and told him I was working out a system for betting on horses. As he can't read, he believed me – and told everyone. Now I have to keep up with the runners and riders, for all my "brothers" ask me for racing tips.

I have at last found a way for Pat to write back to me. When one of us has stolen a little money there's a place we all go to eat on Ninth Avenue. It's called the Roxy Coffee Pot. Mrs Mancini, who makes the coffee, will keep safe any letters that arrive for me until I go in to collect them. She's very kind, though she greets me by pinching my cheek, which hurts, and calls me her *bambino*. She reminds me a little of Mrs Doherty on the ship. She will also post letters for me, so I wrote to Pat telling him to reply to "The Professor", for this is how everyone knows me now.

Saturday 10 November

What am I going to do? I'm so miserable here. I'm covered in bruises, and my hand is so sore that I can hardly hold a pencil.

I've been with this West Side gang more than a week now, and with every moment that passes

I become less happy. Yesterday I decided to do something about it. I'd taken care to let my captors think that I'd joined them willingly. They quickly came to believe that I accepted my new job. Most thought I even enjoyed it, and was becoming – like them – a street urchin.

In fact I was simply waiting for a moment when I could slip away unnoticed. That moment came today. A crowd of us were walking through Paddy's Market (which is what we call the parade of stalls and barrows that spreads out along Ninth Avenue each Saturday night). We were thieving from the stalls. Half of us cause a rumpus to catch the attention of the stall-holders. While they are distracted the other half plunder their display. It's neatly done, but the hawkers aren't fools. When one saw what was happening he shouted for the police. An officer came running and grabbed some of my companions; the rest of us fled in the confusion. This gave me the chance I'd been waiting for. I ran as fast as I could away from Hell's Kitchen.

When I could run no further I stopped and looked around. I was in a big square outside a smart hotel. Above the windows, in gold lettering, was a familiar name: IMPERIAL HOTEL. I took from

my pocket the piece of paper Jack had given me. It was creased and crumpled and the words were barely readable, but they were the same: Imperial Hotel.

I walked over to the front entrance. A tall doorman stood guard, dressed in a smart, heavy coat decorated with gold braid. I gazed at him for a moment, then looked down at my own clothes in shame. I would never get past him in my ragged, filthy outfit. Perhaps he guessed what I was thinking, for he pointed across at me and shouted, "Hey, ragamuffin! Get outta here before I call the cops."

I fled, but his warning gave me an idea. As soon as I saw a policeman, I begged for his help.

What foolishness this was! At first he pretended to be sympathetic when I poured out my story to him. "An orphaned boy?" he said. "Just off the boat…" And, "Trapped into crime, is it?" I trusted him, especially as he was Irish like me. But then I noticed that there was a flicker of a smile on the ends of his mouth as he spoke, which worried me a little, for I'd said nothing amusing.

He took me back to the station house on Thirty-seventh Street, and put me in a room with a cup of tea and a piece of bread. It was spread with some grease and something red and sweet, but without the nice taste that jam has. I could see through the glass of the door as he talked to another cop. There was a lot of nodding with glances in my direction, and thumbs jerked the same way. When the other cop left the station house, the first came back and slid his long truncheon through the door handles of the room where I was sitting. When I complained loudly about this, he withdrew it. Then he came in and beat me on the legs, cursing me all the time. When I recovered from the blows I curled up in the corner and eventually went to sleep.

More blows woke me and I looked up into the angry face of Sly Seamus. He pulled me up by my hair, practically lifting me off the ground, and marched me out past the desk. As he left the station house he shook the hand of the officer who I'd thought would help me and winked at him.

"It's your birthday next week, isn't it, Sean?" he said. Getting a nod back he added, "Well, when you come to collect your cush, we'll stand you a few drinks for returning this lost soul to his family."

Seamus dragged, punched and kicked me the whole way back, telling me all the time what a worthless piece of nonsense I was. He said he'd break every bone in my body if I tried it again. Apparently

I should be grateful to the gang for their protection and the education I'm getting!

Wednesday 14 November

Last Monday, Mike sent me out to sell newspapers. I protested, saying that I'd tried it before and been driven away by other sellers. With a twinkle in his eye, he said, "Don't you worry about that!" and sent me to Newspaper Row with an older lad. Together we collected a hundred papers and took them to a corner to sell. There was already a newsboy selling there, but he fled when we approached.

I sold all my papers, and returned with thirty cents profit. This pleased Mike no end, but it puzzled me. The other lads take ten times this from the pockets of drunks, yet Mike clips them round the ear and tells them to try harder.

Today I found out the reason. As I'd guessed, it has nothing to do with the small profit I'd made. Instead, selling papers is a way of hiding a villain's true trade, which is picking pockets.

I can scarcely believe it, but I'm learning this skill in a real school for pickpockets. In my "class" there are some fifteen boys, most younger than me.

The way we're learning is so like the famous story by Charles Dickens that I joked I should change my name to Oliver Twist. Nobody else found the joke funny. One even asked, "What mob's he in?" I'd forgotten none of them could read.

The way we're learning is like this: we started today with a tailor's dummy, fully dressed as a smart man. And when we have learned to rob this dumb, blind model, we'll advance to robbing our teacher in our basement school room. Only when we're good at it will we go outside to practise our skills on unsuspecting New York people.

Selling papers, it seems, makes stealing easy. Today I learned to use my left hand to wave a paper in the face of whoever I wish to rob, all the while bellowing the headlines in his face. The paper distracts him, and also hides from view the actions of my other hand, which rifles through his pockets.

I learned my lessons poorly. I can't help but look at my right hand as it goes about its wicked business. If my victim was made of flesh and blood, instead of horsehair and sawdust, his eyes would follow my gaze down to his empty pocket, and I would be caught.

Friday 16 November

Walking near a growler shop last night, we saw a drunk lying helpless in the gutter. One of the lads I was with said to me, "Go on – do his pockets!" I refused, but they taunted me. In the end, I thought what I would do if his change had *already* fallen from his pockets and spilled out on the pavement around him. Of course I'd pick it up, for that is just *finding*. How different is it, then, to *help* the money to fall out of the man's pockets? For good measure I took his watch, and Fat Billy gave me two dollars for it! I used the money to buy some new clothes, for mine are grown shiny with grime.

I need to keep these new clothes as clean as I can, for I look halfway respectable in them. I might even get past the doorman of Jack's hotel wearing them.

I dreamed about Ireland last night. I was out ferreting with Pat, only the rabbits that came out of the warren were the size of horses and chased us back to town. I awoke in a sweat and was afraid to shut my eyes again. I lay awake thinking of my da, and how shocked he would be that his son has become a thief.

Saturday 17 November

I am at last becoming a passable pickpocket. Today I succeeded in taking the wallet of Sly Seamus, who teaches us, without him being aware of it. To reward me for my progress, he gave me a valuable tip, which is this: stand close to a sign that says "beware of pickpockets". When they read it, someone carrying valuables will check that they still have them, perhaps by touching the pocket that contains their treasures. To an alert newsboy this is as good as shouting "Rob me!" with the added benefit that he knows which pocket to put his hand in.

Fat Billy has sold the watch that he bought from me. It turned out to be solid gold, and he got far more than the two dollars he paid me. He hasn't told Mike and, to buy our silence, he's promised to treat us all to the show at the Electric theatre on Tenth Avenue and Thirty-seventh Street next week.

Monday 19 November

At last I've had a chance to find out what's happened to Jack! Since I tried to escape, Seamus has made sure that I'm never on my own. If he isn't watching me himself, then he sets an older boy to do it. But today he needed someone to take a package to Eleventh Avenue. There was nobody else to run the errand, so he sent me.

When I'd delivered the parcel, I ran to Jack's hotel. I guessed he was no longer in New York, but I thought the reception clerk might know where he'd travelled on to.

I waited a quarter of an hour on the other side of the road before I plucked up the courage to go in. In my new clothes, I easily slipped past the doorman. Thinking I was a messenger, he simply waved me into the lobby.

At the reception desk, I asked whether they had

a new address for Jack Titchbourne. The clerk stared curiously at my face and started to say, "But aren't *you*...?" Then he gazed at my dirty hands and face, my muddy boots and my uncut hair and tut-tutted.

"The Titchbourne boy and his tutor are still here—" He spun round in his chair— "their key is on the hook, so they can't be in the hotel right now. Are you his brother, or something? Do you have a message for them?"

My heart leaped. I asked for some paper and left a note for Jack. I told him to meet me in the Electric theatre next week, and sit in the back row. Jack is still here! I want to meet him NOW!

Tuesday 20 November

Finally I understand the green goods game. It's not a game at all (I should have guessed!). It's a clever swindle.

Mike began by showing me a printed letter that is sent out to hundreds of thousands of people all over America. These people believe that the letter is offering to sell counterfeit money: false banknotes. The fakes are supposedly so convincing that even a banker cannot tell them from the real thing. A few – very few – people are taken in by the letter. In exchange for five hundred dollars of real money, the mark (or "the sucker" as Mike calls the victim) buys three thousand five hundred dollars in counterfeit notes.

I didn't understand this, so I said to Mike, "If the banknotes are so lifelike, why not spend them yourself?"

To which Mike replied, "Because, my boy, they ain't counterfeit at all, but real moolah."

This confused me more, for I couldn't see how Mike could profit by swapping five hundred dollars for three thousand five hundred dollars.

He rocked back in his chair and smiled. "It's simple. The mark never gets the money home. We swap his bag for one filled with worthless paper."

"What if he finds out and tells the police?"

Mike smiled again. "Now there's the beauty of the game. Because you see, young Professor, what will he say? 'Officer, I went to buy some counterfeit dollars and was swindled.' And anyway, even if he did, what he's just done is illegal."

Again, I wrinkled my brow.

"The law protects only honest men. Suckers caught by the green goods game are breaking the law. So they get what's coming to them."

J.B. Jamison
563 West 36th Street, New York City

Dear Sir,

As you have been recommended to me by one of
my customers as a man who would be likely to
handle a quantity of my goods if the prices suit
you. Now, to be plain, my business is dealing
in denominations of 1s, 2s, 5s and 10s. Do you
understand? If you are willing to enter into
this business with me you must answer this
letter by Telegraph only and I will send you
further information proving to you, to your
entire satisfaction, that you are not taking the
least risk in handling my goods.

If you wish to telegraph under any other name
and address you are at liberty to do so, as I
will not take the liberty of continuing this
correspondence under your own name and address,
unless your telegram reads like this (Send more
information,) and sign name and Post Office
address.

Should you send me a letter instead of a
telegram it will not be received by me, as I
receive communications by Telegraph Only no
matter if your telegraph station is 5 or 10
miles from your home. So if you answer at all
answer as I direct.

Yours in Confidence,

Jamison

I nodded, afraid to appear stupid, but I only really understood hours later, when I'd thought again about every step in the swindle.

Friday 23 November

Once more I spent the day with Mike, but this time I learned exactly what I must do as my part in the trick we're to play.

Mike introduced me to Chalky Miller, who will do the swindle. I will play the part of Chalky's son.

The sucker will be naturally suspicious. Any man would be: he knows he's doing something wrong, and he's spending five-hundred dollars of his own money to do it. My task is to make him less suspicious. I'll travel with him to the railway station, and will sit opposite him while he checks the money in the cab. As Mike says, "He's got Chalky's money and he's got Chalky's son, hasn't he? So of course he trusts Chalky."

At the station, the sucker will post the satchel of money to himself by express, for we shall tell him this is safer than taking it on the train. And at the express office, someone will switch the bags.

"It will be so quick that even *you* won't see it happen," said Mike.

Just as he said this, I had an idea. It was simple, yet it would allow me to escape from Mike and his gang. It would also earn the gratitude, and perhaps a reward, from the mark. Once I'd thought of this, I threw all my energy into the rehearsal of my part in the trick. I knew that my escape depended upon me giving a performance worthy of an actor.

Mike also revealed when the trap will be sprung. The sucker has arranged to travel to the city on Monday 3 December. On that day I'll be free!

Monday 26 November

The flicker that Fat Billy took us to is where the cigar shop on Tenth Avenue used to be. The windows are now painted black, except for a panel in the middle where you can see the machine that throws the pictures. It has a pair of big wheels on top of it. They jerk round when a man cranks a handle on the side. The light shining from the middle of the machine is almost too bright to look at for long. A chimney from the machine blows a faint smell of burning onto the street. There it mixes with the sound of the gramophone that plays all the time from the horn in the doorway.

We stood and stared at the machine while Fat Billy bought eight ten-cent tickets. The woman in the tiny tube-shaped office was suspicious. She wanted to know where Fat Billy had got enough money to pay for us all.

He just smiled sweetly and said, "It's my birthday, miss, and my mom gave it me."

Then thirteen of us ran in so quickly that she didn't have time to count.

Inside, the walls were painted dark red, with signs saying HATS OFF, STAY AS LONG AS YOU LIKE and NO SMOKING. At the front there was a wrinkly bed-sheet nailed to the wall. There were lines of hard chairs laid out, and most of them were empty, so I could see immediately that we'd arrived before Jack. Our crowd nearly filled the front two rows. I made sure that I sat on the second row, at the end.

When the lights went out, a beam of brilliant light coming from the back of the room made moving pictures on the sheet. Though I knew this was what would happen (because it was described to me in Ireland a year ago) I was so startled that I jumped out of my seat. For the man I saw on the screen in front of me was a giant, twice as tall as any real man. Apart from this (and the fact that there's no sound or colour) it was completely lifelike.

As soon as the film started, I turned round to see if Jack had come in, but just at that moment, I felt an elbow in my ribs. Writing had appeared on the screen describing what was happening, and Skinny, who was sitting next to me, hissed, "What does it say, Prof?"

I sat down again impatiently and read off the words as they appeared. Skinny repeated what he'd heard and it was whispered on down the row of seats until everybody knew what was happening.

At the end of the first film, I turned round. There was one person sitting in the back row. It must be Jack! But I had to sit through another motion picture before I could get away. It was accompanied by music on a piano which plays all by itself. Though nobody presses the keys, they go up and down as if invisible fingers are working them! I found this almost as amazing as the motion pictures we came to see.

As soon as the second film finished, the first one started again, but nobody stirred from their seats. I guessed they'd watch both films twice, so I could snatch a good twenty minutes with Jack. I slipped from my seat and crept to the back row.

The first thing Jack said was "Phew! You smell!" and I realized I hadn't had a bath in weeks. Then, "Where have you been? I haven't got much time. Peter will be wondering where I've got to."

I blurted out everything that had happened to me. I told him how miserable I was and how I couldn't escape. When I started, he was impatient, and kept hurrying me up. But as I told him more, he stopped fidgeting and leaned closer to listen. When I'd finished, he said, "Well, you've got to get away – somehow – and come to our hotel. Do you know how to use a telephone?"

I shook my head. He scratched his. Neither of us could think of a plan.

"Why don't we meet here again, when…"

"NO!" I almost shouted it, grabbing Jack's arm. "I can't just get away like that."

Then I had an idea. As quickly as I could, I told him about the green goods game and the sucker on 3 December. "It's exactly a week from today. It'll be late morning. I'll come to your hotel. Please, I'm begging you to help me."

He nodded. "OK. I'll be there."

As he hurried out, I sneaked back to the second row. Nobody had missed me. I hadn't been in my seat for more than a minute before the pictures stopped moving and began to smoke and bubble. There was a rush for the doors, for everyone had heard of fires in electric theatres and we feared we'd cook inside the small room.

Wednesday 28 November

Today we had a grand adventure, brought about because the Thanksgiving festival is but two days away.

We've all been watching hungrily as cart-loads of fat turkeys roll into the city on their way to slaughter.

One of our brothers hatched a plan, "so that we might all eat as well as the finest New Yorker in a couple of days."

We stationed ourselves at a crossroads and, by banging bins, caused a horse to shy just as a big turkey wagon approached. This stopped all the traffic and we clambered aboard and burst open the cages it carried. I think the plan was to capture and eat the birds. I was to earn my keep by showing them all how to kill, pluck and gut a turkey.

Unfortunately, nobody had bothered to explain the plan to the turkeys. Instead of meekly submitting to us, they took off at a cracking pace, all in different directions. Though each of us chose our turkey, and sprinted after it, they all escaped into the alleyways and tenements, and we returned hungry.

I think it's probably lucky that they escaped, for we'd not planned how we were going to cook the birds. Of course none of us has an oven.

Friday 30 November: Thanksgiving

My first thought when I woke up was dismay that we wouldn't be eating roast turkey. I asked my companions where we might find something else to eat today.

"Don't worry!" they all said. "Thanksgiving is the one day of the year when we all stuff ourselves with food."

My eyes opened wide like saucers. "So why were we chasing turkeys two days ago, then?" I asked.

"Why, Prof! Ain't you got no brains? To sell, of course!" answered Fat Billy.

"And for the sport of it!" chimed Mutton-Head Mo.

I found out that we'd eat in the afternoon at some

197

secret place they'd take me to. Before that we took a trip downtown. My chums amused themselves no end by refusing to say where we were going. Despite my begging and pleading they wouldn't tell me what was happening.

Eventually, we halted on a crowded pavement and waited – but not for long. First I heard a distant cheering, with the occasional musical note. Before long, the odd notes joined up to make a proper tune.

When I realized that it was a marching band, panic and fright filled me up in case it turned out to be an Orange parade. I struggled to escape, but the people behind me pressed forward so hard that I couldn't even move my arms.

To my relief there was no trace of orange. Instead, it was a collection of people like I'd never seen before. Behind the marching band came The Original Hounds, a crowd of rowdy men, red-nosed and riding in ancient carts drawn by bony horses almost as old.

Behind *them* marched a great crowd in fancy dress. There were cowboys and Indians, and others in brilliantly coloured costumes imitating the fashions of the past. Among them were "Fantastics" – men dressed as women – who cavorted along to cheers from bystanders.

When the Hounds had gone past we rushed a couple of blocks to view another parade, so in rapid turn I watched the Mackerel Rangers, the Woodstock Guards, the Frog Swamp Rangers and the Lily White Ducks. Best of all, we could join in these festivities, tagging along behind and collecting pennies in our caps. I had more than two dollars by the time the parades had ended.

There was better to come, but I was teased some more before I was allowed to enjoy it. We headed for Chinatown, where I was told we would be visiting Wing Lee's grocery store. Sure enough, when we reached Doyers Street, that's what the sign said above number fifteen. But a door at the side led up to the second floor, where the Rescue Mission has its home.

When we first lined up with our plates there was a lot of shoving to be at the front. However, as soon as it became clear that there was no shortage of food, my gang behaved better and there was a great deal of sarcastic, "No, after *you*, Professor," as they made fun of my accent and what they think are polite manners.

Piled high, my plateful was all I could eat, but there was no limit on seconds, and some went back for more – a few even ate three helpings. To follow there was Christmas pudding (which everyone here calls "plum" pudding) and ice cream – as if it were summer!

After the meal, there was a church service, and I was astonished to see everyone put their hands together and bow their heads. For those who didn't pray (or at least act as if they were) wouldn't get to see the jinx and jollities after.

I really *did* pray. The trick I'd learned from Mike is to be sprung on Saturday, and I prayed that I would be able to escape as planned.

Monday 3 December

I should have been free today, but I'm still a prisoner! Worse for my soul, I fear I can no longer tell right from wrong.

The green goods game, which Mike had trained me so carefully for, ran exactly as he said it would. The sucker arrived on time at the hotel room we'd rented. He was sweating, though the room wasn't warm. He kept running his hand round the inside of his collar, as if it fitted him badly, or was stiffer than he was used to. When he arrived he glared at me and growled, "Why's he here?" Chalky explained that my mother was ill, so he had to look after me for the day. After that I had to do little more than watch.

The mark showed his money, and Chalky showed his, and the mark looked at it very carefully. "They're good," he said, "*Very* good."

"Would you like to take some to a bank to change them, and assure yourself that they'll fool a teller?" Chalky asked.

"That won't be necessary," he replied, "for I'm a teller myself."

This made Chalky hesitate for the first time. His patter up until now had been as smooth as silk. "You're a teller? How did you come by five hundred dollars on a teller's salary?"

Now it was the mark's turn to be nervous. "I ... I've *borrowed* the money. But of course I'll return it to the bank tomorrow."

He turned back to gaze at the satchel full of money, with wide eyes. He could hardly wrench his eyes away from it. Chalky winked at me. Then the mark handed over his own wad of money, closed the satchel and hugged it to his belly. He dabbed his brow with his sleeve.

"How do I know I can trust you? You may have paid a villain to rob me on the way back to Grand Central."

Chalky spread his hands apart with the palms up. "I'm an honest man," he said, opening his coat wide. "Look, I'm unarmed, but I see you're less trusting."

This made the mark more uncomfortable still, for even I could see the shiny new revolver pushed into the waistband of his trousers.

"Look, if you're so worried, my son will go with you to the station," said Chalky, and this was my signal to repeat the line I'd learned.

"Can we go in a motor cab?" I asked with mock excitement.

"Why, of course!" said my "father". "And in the cab you can watch while this gentleman checks his money, for he seems to think we might switch it for a brick."

This last line was the cleverest of all, for it was *exactly* what the sucker suspected we'd do. Reassured, he relaxed his grip on the bag a little and we went downstairs.

Now *I* became nervous. I'd decided that once inside the cab I'd reveal the plot to the mark, and ask him to take me to Jack's hotel. There he could escape with the money, and I'd be free at last.

The doorman called a motor cab over and we got in. I made sure that the mark sat so that the driver wouldn't see him open the bag. And of course, this is just what he did as soon as we set off.

As he looked at the money I began the speech I'd prepared.

"I think you should know…" I began, but I stopped because he didn't look up, as I expected he would. He was just gazing at the money.

He pulled out a note and ran his fingers gently across it.

I hadn't expected this.

He raised a twenty-dollar bill to his nose, sniffed at it and smiled. He was so excited that he didn't see me or hear me, though I was right in front of him.

Suddenly I began to see him just as Mike and Chalky did: "They get what they deserve." Chalky was right.

I also realized that I'd never persuade him to take me to Jack's hotel. He hardly knew I was there. Even shouting at him might not break the spell that the cash had cast over him. If it did, why would he take the advice of a boy?

So we rode on in silence to the station. There, the mark gripped my wrist so tightly that I cried out in pain, and hurried me to the express office. Once we were inside I did what I'd been told to do. I stood next to him on the other side from his bag. Until then he'd kept it gripped tightly in his hand. Now, though, he had to put it down so that he could reach for his wallet. Just at that moment, Seamus barged past, almost knocking me to the ground. He stopped and apologized elaborately, and even bent down and shook my hand. I pretended he was a stranger.

By the time this little act was over, the mark had his wallet in his hand, so he bent down and picked up his precious bag again. Except that now, it *wasn't* his bag. The bag with the money in it had a tiny scratch on the front. *This bag* lacked the scratch. In his greed and haste, he didn't notice this.

The mark stepped up to the counter and gave the clerk his address. When he took the receipt and turned round, he shouted at me.

"Why are you still here? Get on with you!" He aimed a kick at me and I ran from the office. Seamus was waiting for me outside, and we took the subway back to Hell's Kitchen. My silence and solemn look made Seamus ask me, "What's eating you, kid?" but of course I couldn't tell him that I'd just missed my best chance to escape.

Wednesday 5 December

Today I was selling papers on the Weehawken ferry that leaves from the end of Forty-second Street. This isn't a pitch that newsboys fight over, because sales aren't good there. Seamus had decided that it was a good place for me to learn to pick pockets with little chance of capture. He thinks I'll make a fine "moll-buzzer" – stealing from women – because he says I have an innocent smile, and my pockmarked face means ladies feel sorry for me!

When I started on the ferry yesterday, Mutton-Head Mo came with me, but today I was allowed to ride to and fro on my own. Of course, my first thought was that after a single there-and-back trip I could slip away to the Imperial Hotel, find Jack and hide up with him there. But I soon saw that what seemed like a simple plan wasn't going to be easy. Mutton-Head Mo sells the *Journal* at the end of Forty-second Street. I couldn't leave the ferry without him seeing me, and he'd want to know where I was going. My clothes are also filthy again, for I slid over yesterday in the street outside the slaughterhouse. The hotel doorman wouldn't even need to see me to bar my way: he would smell me coming. And finally I'm ashamed that I didn't turn up at the hotel on Saturday as I arranged with Jack, though surely he'd forgive me that – if he hasn't left already. So I did nothing and miserably sold papers for a day in the cold Hudson River breeze.

Friday 7 December

Today has been truly the most extraordinary day of my life. I've had an amazing surprise – and a dreadful, tragic shock. I escaped – but now I'm a prisoner again, though in quite a different way. And (not for the first time) my world has been turned completely upside down. I'm writing this in clean, pressed clothes, at a proper desk, by electric light, in the warmth and comfort of a hotel room.

Today began much like any other day since I moved to the West Side. I picked up a hundred *Journals* and took them down to the pier to sell on the ferry. I'd made several trips to Weehawken and back. I'd just tried to pull a leather from a man's pocket when he looked down. Thinking he had caught sight of my hand dipping, I fled along the deck.

However, my feet were faster than my head, for as I rushed around a corner, I ran straight into someone coming the other way. I was knocked to the ground, and lay there a moment trying to catch my breath. When I did, all I could think of was my pile of papers. The wind had caught them, and they were blowing about and hanging on the deck rails like laundry. I'd only sold half a dozen, and taken nothing from anyone's pockets. If I lost all I'd brought to sell I would have just a few cents left.

As I scrambled to pick up the *Journals*, a voice above me shouted, "DAVID!"

Nobody calls me this any more, for I am "Prof" to my mob, so I jumped at hearing my name. I put my foot on the papers I'd herded into a rough pile, and looked up. It was Jack!

For an instant we gazed at each other, saying nothing. Then he demanded to know what I was doing here on the Weehawken ferry. I asked him the same question.

When we'd last met in the darkness of the Electric theatre, Jack had been little more than a shadow. In daylight it was clear that we looked less alike than we had on the *Campania*. If we were brothers, then Jack was the brother who'd prospered, and I was the one who had fallen on hard times. My clothes were thin and grimy; he looked like a New York gentleman in miniature. He was dressed for the winter, in a heavy coat.

He helped me pick up my papers, and we found a place out of the wind. And there, as the ferry plied

back and forth, we talked for an hour.

To start with, he gazed at me through narrowed eyes.

"Where *were* you on Saturday?" he asked accusingly. "I had to tell Peter such lies so that we could stay at the hotel all morning. And then you didn't show up!"

So I told him everything. When we met at the Electric, I'd only had time to babble out the briefest description of my time in New York. Now he heard every detail. Some I'm sure he didn't believe, and his eyes opened so wide that I thought they'd drop out onto his lap.

He had less to tell. "I've slipped away…" he began. "Remember I told you on the *Campania* that I'd be staying in a hotel with Peter? Well, our stay has lasted much longer than we expected. My father and his wife were supposed to come from the Mid-West a month ago to pick me up, but they were held up…"

He explained that his stepmother had been taken ill, and couldn't travel. To begin with this wasn't a problem. "Peter and I just lived at the Imperial Hotel. It's comfortable, but not expensive. We ate there; they washed our clothes and cleaned the room. It was just boring."

Peter had to return to Britain to teach at a school. So when Jack's stepmother was well again, his father had arranged to bring the whole family to New York to meet Jack. They'd expected to arrive yesterday, just hours before Peter's steamer sailed for Liverpool.

But this morning a cable arrived. A storm had flooded the railroad tracks, and they'd be delayed a further day. Jack took it from his pocket and showed it to me.

"LEAVE JACK C/O IMPERIAL. ETA NYC 10PM FRIDAY," I read aloud. "What's C/O? And ETA?" I knew what NYC was.

"'Care of' and 'estimated time of arrival'," Jack explained, drumming his fingers on the greasy table.

"Ten o'clock Friday? That's tonight," I said.

He grinned. "Yes! I have another seven hours of freedom to do … well, just about anything I want to. I wasn't supposed to leave the hotel, but I sneaked out of the staff entrance."

"But why are you going to Weehawken?" I asked. "There's nothing much to see there."

"I wanted to see the Hudson River, so I walked west. Then I saw the cliffs and the ferry … and I had nothing better to do…"

I was amazed he'd walked through Hell's Kitchen without being robbed.

We'd reached the Forty-second Street pier again, so we got off. We evaded Mutton-Head Mo with the simplest of tricks: Jack bought a paper, and dropped change to distract him while I hurried past behind him.

I was famished, so Jack bought me a sandwich. It was salt beef, and cost as much as I earn from selling papers for a whole day.

He was silent as I sat eating it, then said, "Come back to the hotel. You can come and live with us. I'm sure there'd be something we could find for you to do."

211

The idea alarmed me, and I shook my head, remembering Seamus's warning that he'd find me anywhere. I told Jack about the last time I tried to escape, and how even the police did nothing to protect me.

"Don't worry: you could hide up until we left New York. Then you'd be a thousand miles away."

I thought about it, and found myself looking over my shoulder cautiously. There was nobody listening to our conversation.

"All right," I whispered. I still feared Seamus's spies.

"Come on, then!" Jack got up.

I went to follow him, but then I noticed how well he was dressed. I looked down at my own clothes. "They'd never let me in the hotel like this!"

So we decided to split up. Jack would go back to the hotel to get some clothes for me, whilst I returned to the cellar to pick up what little I owned. We arranged to meet up again, but off the street. I showed him the place. It was nearby, under a wharf. You walk down a slipway, and lift away a loose grating. It's a tight squeeze, even for a boy, but once you're through you can walk upright balancing on the big pier timbers, dodging the dock machinery. At high tide, the water washes over your feet, but it's safe if you know where to step.

When I got back to the cellar, Roper, one of the bigger boys from our mob, was there. He took one look at me and asked, "Why ain't you out selling?" Looking at my papers he said, "Why've you got so many left? What's happened to them? They're not fit to sell. Have you found anything yet?"

"I got stopped by a market trader and accused of thieving fruit. He called the police and it was the best I could do to get away at all." He nodded, but not like he really believed it.

I pretended to be looking for something in my bag while he watched me from a corner. Then, as soon as he shuffled up the stairs, I frantically packed everything I could into my pockets. I'd even less to carry than when I fled from Cherry Street. More of my belongings had been stolen, sold, pawned, borrowed and not returned, or torn into strips for bandages. This time even my da's watch had gone. I'd hidden it behind a loose brick, but maybe someone had watched me, or noticed that the wall was uneven. To my relief, though, nobody was interested in my journal.

I sneaked out the back way, but this wasn't enough to hide my escape. At the end of the alley I saw a figure against the light. As I spotted him, he turned. He started down the alley after me. I ran.

It had just begun to snow, big fluffy flakes that stuck to my cold clothes. I sprinted as fast as I could, my breath bursting from my mouth and making great white clouds in the cold air before me. I ducked down every alley I knew, but my pursuer knew them, too.

And now there were two of them. I ran and ran. I could smell the oily river ahead of me. Then I could hear it lapping, though the urgent, frightening sound of feet slapping in the wet snow behind me was louder.

I *had* to meet Jack. It was the only way I could escape, and I was already late.

I darted down the slipway. Struggling past the grating, I caught my trousers on a nail and tore away half the leg. I pressed myself into a curve in the culvert beyond as the two figures dashed past the grille.

"I'm sure he ran down this slip."

"Sshh! Just be quiet for a minute and listen."

I held my breath in the darkness, but still there was a loud regular thumping in my ears. I was terrified they'd hear it, too.

The pair searched for half an hour. They even stared into the culvert. I was freezing and had to grab my jaw to stop my chattering teeth from giving me away. When I heard them slink away, I walked on through the shadows.

I was late. I guessed it was an hour after we'd said we'd meet. I'd looked up at a clock on the ferry-pier building as I ran, and I was twenty minutes late even then. But Jack wasn't here. Maybe he'd been and gone? I searched around in the fading light. Arc lamps popped into life high above my head. They cast brilliant blue-white bars across everything, making it even more difficult to see into the shadows. When I'd looked everywhere, I looked again. I even whistled – a hoot that I thought might catch Jack's attention, but not that of the workers just a foot or two above my head.

Finally I found him, lying below some huge cog wheels that moved a crane on the wharf above. My first thought was, *He can't be sleeping, not here in this cold?*

"Jack?"

Sure enough, he was stretched out on a wide beam, peaceful, with his eyes tight shut.

"JACK!"

As I got close enough to see his face, I suddenly wasn't sure. It was Jack, but somehow it wasn't. Jack always had a smile twisting up the corners of his mouth, even when he was serious. Now his face was blank and slack. His leg was twisted round under him in the most peculiar, uncomfortable way. That's when I realized.

My stomach heaved: salt beef, milk and rye bread splattered into the Hudson.

I knelt over him. A thread of dark stickiness trickled from his head and dripped into the water. I turned him over. Low on the back of his skull was a hole: neat, deep, round and black. Besides blood, something grey oozed from it. I shivered, and leaned down to puke again.

Just at that moment the machine above me sprung into life with a clattering mechanical growl. From the corner of my eye I caught sight of something moving quickly. I felt the breeze lift my hair as a great iron arm swung past. This was what had happened to Jack. From where he was wounded I guessed he'd been sitting up.

I curled myself into a ball a safe distance away and pressed my back into one of the splintery oak columns. For perhaps half an hour I watched the mechanism swing back and forth about Jack's lifeless shape. Then I heard the engine cut out above my head, and the massive arm drifted slowly to a halt.

I *had* to go and tell Jack's parents about this dreadful thing that had happened to my friend. But how would I find them? And how would I get into the hotel? I went through Jack's pockets and found his key and a couple of dollar bills, then I looked around for the clothes he said he'd bring for me. He hadn't forgotten them: I could see a bag in the water. It was scarcely afloat, and the ebbing tide had sucked it out of reach.

There was only one way I'd get past the hotel doorman. I started to strip Jack's clothes from his body. It was awkward. Several times I almost fell in, and I nearly lost his jacket in the water, too. Finally, though, I slipped into his outfit. It was grim to wear his clothes, but I was grateful for the warmth of the thick wool coat.

As I pocketed the key, I heard voices.

"He must have gone in there! I'll never get through. Fetch one of the ragamuffins." The voice was unmistakable: it was Seamus.

The iron grille was the only way out. I waited, shivering in the cold. I could hear Seamus pacing outside the grille. Snow drifted through the boards above my head. Then silence. I waited ten more minutes and crept gingerly out. I put my head through the culvert and looked left and right. There were some footprints in the snow, but no sign of Seamus. I squeezed through.

"Hey! There he is! Prof! Get over here! I wanna word with you!"

The shouting came from above my head. Seamus was on the wharf above me, with two of the boys. I fled down Thirty-third Street, then turned south on Eleventh Avenue, away from Hell's Kitchen, but they were too quick. I knew they'd run me down within a block. I ran across the railway tracks and darted round a corner … straight into the arms of a policeman.

Sly Seamus was on me in a second, tugging at Jack's new jacket. "Come on, Prof! Don't waste my time."

The policeman pulled us apart, looking curiously at my clothes. "What's this about?" He narrowed his eyes and stared at Seamus. "Haven't I seen you at the station house?"

Seamus planted both feet wide apart and pointed a filthy finger at me. Despite the cold, his face was bright red. "He belongs to me. He's coming with us."

Terror gripped me by the throat as tightly as the policeman held my collar. He gazed down at me and wrinkled his brow. "What have you got to say to that, son?"

Unless I said something, I'd be back with Sly Seamus and his mob of grimy thieves. I'd probably get another beating, too. I opened my mouth to speak, but no sound came out. Then, suddenly, I had a brilliant idea.

I turned my face up to the policeman. With all the confidence I could muster, I said, "Officer, there has been a terrible mistake. I am Jack Titchbourne. I do not know this man. I want to return to the Imperial Hotel, where I am staying."

The cop relaxed his grip on me. "Is that so?" I pulled the Imperial key from my pocket and held it up.

"No way!" Seamus's eyes were wide with rage and disbelief. "It's a lie!"

The cop pushed him away. "Shove off!" Then he turned back to me. "That's only three blocks away. We'll soon see if you're telling the truth…"

At the reception desk I pulled Jack's cap down to hide as much of my face as I dared, but I needn't have bothered.

220

I had Jack's clothes; I had Jack's key; I had Jack's face. For all the desk clerk knew, I *was* Jack.

And that is how I came to be writing this at the Imperial Hotel. For now, I'm safe, but in a few hours Jack's parents will arrive, and I must tell them their son is dead. What will they do? Will they help me escape from New York? I'm dreading meeting them.

Monday 10 December

Jack's ma and pa arrived late at night and crept into the room. I wasn't asleep, but I pretended to be. When they returned the following morning I was planning to say, "There's something I have to tell you: I'm not Jack…" but I got no further than the second word before Jack's stepmother stopped me with a hug. When she sat back and said, "Let me look at you! Heavens, you are the spit of your father…" I realized that explaining what had happened was going to be even more difficult than I'd imagined.

Then it was Jack's father's turn. He shook me by the hand and I started again:

"Sir, I…"

But once more, I got no further, for he interrupted me.

"Pop! Call me Pop. You're not in Europe any more. We're not formal like that over here. Go on: call me Pop."

So I said, "Good morning … Pop."

This was my first, biggest and most difficult lie. Afterwards, the lies got easier, and telling the truth became more and more impossible with each minute that passed.

They asked me many questions – about Ireland, the crossing, and about my time in New York. I lied as if my life depended on it – which, in a way, I suppose it did. I told them everything Jack had told me. I was glad I'd listened carefully and paid attention during those long hours we'd spent together on the ship. I was careful, very careful, not to make anything up. I knew that if I did, I could easily be trapped by my inventions. When they asked me a question I couldn't answer I just pretended I'd forgotten. Sometimes I answered another question altogether.

By the time the day ended I realized that nobody would believe me if I told them who I really was.

I must stop here, because I have just half an hour on my own before we take the train out West. This will be the last entry I write, for this journal has become a terrible danger to me. Because, it seems, I have *become* my dear friend Jack Titchbourne. *His* family has become *my* family. *His* life is now *my* life. And David O'Connor, who until yesterday wrote this journal, is floating cold and lifeless in the Hudson River.

I have written a note to Pat and am sending this journal to him to destroy. He needs to know what's happened. I will never forget him, but he must forget David O'Connor, whose story ends here.

Afterword   by Richard Platt

I was lucky enough to buy this remarkable diary five years ago in a secondhand shop when I was on holiday in County Cavan.

A demolition contractor had sold it to the shop, along with some other bric-a-brac. He had found the book hidden under an inch of dust, in the loft of a derelict mansion that he was pulling down.

The shop's owner had barely glanced at it, and thought it was worthless.

I disagreed. When I got the book back to my hotel and began reading, I couldn't stop. I turned the last page at three in the morning. What I discovered between the worn, curling covers was quite simply the most astonishing story I had ever read.

Over the next few weeks, I checked every detail. In newspaper archives, I found David's obituary, which I have stuck in over the page. I also learned a lot about Patrick. When his father died, he took over the family draper's shop where he had worked since leaving school without qualifications. For years he lived modestly, but his fortunes changed soon after he sold the shop and retired. He bought Bellamont Forest, a large mansion nearby. If asked where he found the money to do this, he would say only, "I came by it honestly."

Pat died seven years after his friend, and the mansion crumbled while his children argued over who should have it. Pat took David's secret to the grave, but (thankfully) did not obey David's request to destroy the diary after reading it.

I have thought long and hard about what to do with this fantastic book. In the end, I decided that, since both David and Pat are long dead, publishing it would harm no one. It is an extraordinary tale, and I hope you have enjoyed reading it.

Richard Platt
London, June 2010

TYCOON'S LAST WILL AND TESTAMENT READ

Titchbourne leaves his multi-billion-dollar fortune to charity.

FAMILY LEFT OUT

The Last Will and Testament of American tycoon John D. Titchbourne was published yesterday. As had been widely predicted, the industrialist left the bulk of his $11.4 billion fortune to charities and good causes he supported in his lifetime.

Titchbourne rose to prominence in the 1950s through shrewd business deals that gave him control of a large part of the American steel industry. He had an uncanny knack for anticipating bear and bull markets, buying and selling stocks with well-timed judgement, so that his name came to stand for supernatural foresight: "a touch of Titchbourne" was a compliment paid to charmed investors who saw boom or bust coming.

MYSTERY OF ORIGINS

Though he came from a family of wealthy New Jersey industrialists, Titchbourne spent much of his early childhood with relatives in Ireland, following the death of his mother. This formative experience gave his speech a slight Irish accent that he never quite lost. Of his childhood, and about most other details of his early life, Titchbourne was tight-lipped to the point of secrecy. Journalists and investigators who tried to find out more were at the very least

> Turn to page 22

Acknowledgements

I owe a debt of gratitude to all these people, who together helped to make *Double Crossing* a far better book.

The editors and designers at Walker, for their hard work, and constant and unswerving help and encouragement.

Charles H. Smith, Professor and Science Librarian, Department of Library Public Services, Western Kentucky University, for his help in tracking down Alfred Russel Wallace's writings about vaccination.

Drew Keeling, economic historian at the University of Zurich, who gave me details of steerage on the *Campania*.

Michael Corcoran, at Ireland's National Transport Museum, and Manus McGuirk at the Dublin and Irish Local Studies Collection of Dublin

City Library, for their help with the minutiae of the Dublin tram network.

Kieran Murphy of Murphy's Ice Cream, Dingle, for his information about ice cream in early 20th-century Ireland.

Kenneth Cobb of the New York City Municipal Archives, for his help in tracing the history of the Green Goods Business.

Michael Coleman professor of English at the University of Jyväskylä, Finland, for his help on the Irish school year.

The staff of the Liverpool Maritime Museum, for helping me with information, memorabilia and deck plans of the *Campania*.

The real Liam and Susan, for their special help.

Flip by Martyn Bedford

Fourteen-year-old Alex Gray wakes up one morning to discover he's not in his own bedroom. More surprising is that he doesn't recognize his hands, or his legs... When he looks in the mirror he gets the shock of his life! How is it possible that Alex has become another boy – a boy who everyone calls Philip? And how have six whole months passed overnight? A riveting psychological thriller by a brilliant new voice in children's books.

ISBN 978-1-4063-4423-3 • £6.99

Wild Boy by Rob Lloyd Jones

Wild Boy has been covered in hair since birth; he's the missing link, a monster, a sideshow spectacle. Condemned to life in a travelling freakshow, excluded from society and abused by his master, he takes refuge in watching people come and go at the fair – and develops a Sherlock Holmes style talent for observation and detection. But when there's a murder, suspicion turns on Wild Boy, and he and the feisty redhaired acrobat Clarissa Everett find themselves on the run from a London-wide manhunt. Together, the detective and the acrobat must solve clues to identify the real killer.

ISBN 978-1-4063-4776-0 • £9.99

Monkey Wars by Richard Kurti

When the Langur monkey troop rises to power on the dusty streets of Calcutta, it is at a price. A brutal massacre drives the Rhesus troop out of the place they called home and forces them to embark on a dangerous journey. But one Langur monkey, Mico, is prepared to stand up to the tyrannical Langur regime and fight for truth, friendship and love. As Mico uncovers the secrets and lies at the heart of the corrupt Langur leadership, he quickly realizes he is playing a dangerous game. And when monkeys turn on each other, there can be no survivors...

ISBN 978-1-4063-4882-8 • £7.99

Vango by Timothée de Fombelle

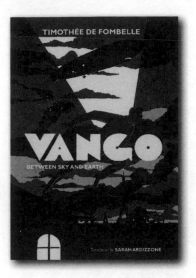

Raised by a strange nanny in Sicily, Vango grows up with one friend, a priest Zefiro, who lives in a monastery hidden from sight. On reaching adulthood, Vango decides to follow in Zefiro's steps, but at the moment he is taking his holy orders at Notre Dame in Paris, he is falsely accused of a crime and has to go on the run. This is a breathless and highly cinematic story that follows Vango travelling by Zeppelin across Europe from Stromboli to Nazi Germany, from Scotland to the Soviet Union, climbing the rooftops of Paris, crossing the paths of arms traffickers, crooked policemen, Russian spies and even Stalin.

ISBN 978-1-4063-3092-2 • £9.99

For Mary

First published 2010 by Walker Books Ltd
87 Vauxhall Walk, London SE11 5HJ

2 4 6 8 10 9 7 5 3 1

Text © 2010 Richard Platt
Illustrations © 2010 Alexandra Higlett

This edition published 2013

River scene print © Swim Ink 2, LLC/Corbis.
Map of New York reprinted by permission of Encyclopædia Britannica, Inc.
Obituary photograph © Mary Evans Picture Library/
Classic Stock/H. Armstrong Roberts.
Images of the passenger log book and inspection card are reproduced
by permission of Gjenvick-Gjønvik Archives

The right of Richard Platt and Alexandra Higlett to be
identified as author and illustrator respectively of this
work has been asserted by them in accordance with the
Copyright, Designs and Patents Act 1988

This book has been typeset in Granjon

Printed and bound in Great Britain by Clays Ltd, St Ives plc

British Library Cataloguing in Publication Data:
a catalogue record for this book is available from the British Library

ISBN 978-1-4063-4505-6

www.walker.co.uk